Henry Brereton Marriott Watson

At the First Corner

And other Stories

Henry Brereton Marriott Watson

At the First Corner
And other Stories

ISBN/EAN: 9783744751421

Printed in Europe, USA, Canada, Australia, Japan

Cover: Foto ©Andreas Hilbeck / pixelio.de

More available books at **www.hansebooks.com**

AT THE FIRST CORNER

AND OTHER STORIES

At the First Corner

AND OTHER STORIES BY

H. B. Marriott Watson

AUTHOR OF
'DIOGENES OF LONDON'

London : John Lane, Vigo St.
Boston : Roberts Bros., 1895

CONTENTS

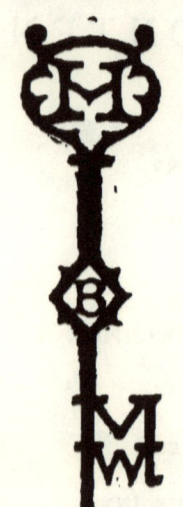

AT THE FIRST CORNER

MILLICENT stood awhile with her hand on the door. Now that she had come so far she was disposed to turn back. A medley of superficial sensations swarmed within her. She flushed warm, and then a quick chill took her; excitement fluttered in her heart; she felt the great stream of light from the fanlight in the hall play over her face pleasantly; and at the last arose a sudden fear. A certain feeling of resentment too separated itself from among the conflicting emotions, and was individualised distinctly for a moment. She wondered if she had not better put off the task until she were more in her own control; but to this mood succeeded the thought that she must bring the news sometime, and that concealment would fret her. She opened the door and went in.

Rossiter looked up as the lock snapped, and half-turning in his chair put his arms over his head towards her. 'If it were an invitation she ignored it, standing by him in silence. He smiled in her face.

'Finished all your work, little woman?' he asked, stretching himself. 'Taking a spell? You have interrupted a most desultory piece of verse. I have no inspiration this morning. I can't get the last two lines right. The first verse is decent.

> The grey clouds gathered in the skies,
>   And loud the west wind blew
> With gusty sobs and long-drawn sighs,
>   And all for me and you.
> It wailed round roof and tree, my dear ;
>   Too well its word I knew—
> Farewell 'twixt you and me, my dear,
>   Farewell 'twixt me and you.

The feeling I want to get is that all things really shadowed my trouble, and were not, what they were as a matter of fact, ordinary natural phenomena. But I can't phrase it.'

'What was your trouble?' she asked.

'Parting, dear—the sudden knowledge of a collapse, the most tragic accident in life. Isn't that so?' She leaned over him and looked at the paper on which he had been writing; he put up a hand and caught hold of her arm.

She rested her chin upon his head in an absent manner.

'I suppose so,' she said listlessly, 'I've not gone through it.'

'Nor have I, Milly. But can't you imagine it? Don't you know what it would be if we were to part?'

'Oh, yes.'

He looked at her inquiringly, and his eyes fell. A tiny sigh escaped him, and for an instant his face was wried with a clutch of pain. 'I wonder what you would forgive,' he said. 'I wonder if your love is strong enough to forgive much.'

'You know that I am not very jealous by nature.'

He made an angry movement.

'Pah! I don't mean sordid things like that. You hurt me. I should never ask you to forgive that. Good God, what do you mean by saying you're not jealous? If you're not, you can't care a rap—you—Milly, you make me miserable.'

She laughed softly. 'I'm sorry, my dear boy. You know I'm fond of you. Wasn't it proof enough when I gave up my own good name for you? It was very injudicious, I suppose.'

'You don't regret it?' he asked anxiously.

'I never regretted it; no,' she returned slowly; 'but——'

'What?' he said under his breath.

'Oh, nothing,' she exclaimed with some impatience; 'nothing, nothing.'

She moved away. Once more the fear returned to her, and the little cloud of anger gathered in her heart. She did not know how to tell him, and yet she had even a desire to hurt him in the telling. He watched her with distressed eyes.

'Milly,' he pleaded; 'you did not mind leaving your uncle and coming to me?'

'It was necessary, I suppose, since I was so impulsive. I wasn't wise enough to wait for your wife's death; and apparently I should be waiting still.'

He winced as though a hand had struck him.

'Would you have sooner waited?' he asked in tones barely audible. She did not answer. 'Milly, are you sorry you did not wait?' he repeated.

'Oh, what is the use of talking? I don't

know. It's done with now, and we can't go back.'

He laid down his pen, and the hand that held it was trembling.

'I always was selfish,' he said sadly.

'No, it was not your fault. It was mine. I was a fool in impulse. What sort of creature was I five years ago?'

'You were very charming,' he answered softly.

'Did you like me better then than now?'

'Now, now—ten thousand times now,' he said. And rising suddenly, he put his arms round her. She smiled, and leaned her face against his.

'That is flattering to a woman—and I think I've developed my vanity lately.'

'Is the life too dull for you, dear? Do you want more friends? I've sometimes fancied it must be.'

'I don't know. Do I? I don't think so. I don't know. Perhaps I do.'

She answered vacantly. She did not know; she was conscious merely of unrest and that growing resentment.

'I hate to be shackled,' she burst out.

'Darling,' he said in dismay, 'you are not shackled. You are not bound to me, even as tightly as I could wish you bound.'

'I am, I am,' she cried, and stamped her foot with sudden passion.

He stood silent, discomfited.

'Are you ill, dear?' he asked tenderly.

'Yes, yes,' she murmured.

'What is it? A headache? Do lie down, and I'll get you some sal volatile.'

She laughed somewhat harshly, 'Oh, it's not going to be cured by sal volatile. It's more serious than that, much more damnable. I hate it,' she cried. 'I hate it,' and a sob rose in her throat.

His eyes dilated with sudden understanding ; the lines of his mouth tightened, and then as swiftly relaxed ; a shade of horror flitted across his face.

'Is it so?' he whispered. 'Is it really so, dear?' She flamed red ; her eyes flashed with some evil temper. 'It is you ; it is you who have done this,' she said ; and with a cry half of passion and half of pain, she fled from the room. Rossiter remained with his eyes upon the floor, the look of disquiet twisting his

handsome features askew.   Then he sat down
in his chair and picked up his pen.

> ' I saw the sobbing river flow,
>   I saw the sweeping rain ;
> The wet vine, tossing to and fro,
>   Flapped loose upon the pane.
> I looked out o'er the lea, my dear,
>   And all too well I knew
> They wept for you and me, my dear,
>   They wept for me and you.'

He hid his face in the hollows of his hands and
sighed. Raising himself he looked at his verses,
but it was not the rhymes that held his attention.
From the experiments upon the page one word
leapt out and struck him fiercely, as it had been
a flash of lightning. ' Cheat' swam in his vision
and sounded in his ears.   The room buzzed
with it.   But at this moment, with the echoes
of her voice still calling from the corners, the
pain of his humiliation was become twofold.
All these years he had locked the sullen spectre
in his heart, from which it had escaped at
intervals to gibe and mock at him.   He had
endured the agony of one fear these five years
—the fear of shame, and shame alone ; and now
must there be added also the horror of despair ?
He had been afraid that she should know with

how little love he had begun, how slight a risk
he had taken, how lightly he had regarded her.
But if she had begun to grow cold, if the
temper of her affection had altered, he must
take a new burden upon him. Surely she
could not have ceased to love him ; surely this
caprice of anger, of indifference, merely issued
from the derangement of her nerves, from a
temporary indisposition.

Since he had come to love her and seen
thereby the monstrous disloyalty of his sin,
Rossiter had never denied to himself the gross-
ness of his selfish nature. She was but twenty
when he had tempted her—a wayward and
impulsive girl with quick instincts of affection.
He had played the coward when she deemed
him to be enacting the hero. Her face attracted
him, her voice enchanted him ; but the irre-
vocability of marriage frightened him. He was
by nature too indulgent to his own whims to
withdraw from the sphere of her fascinations ;
and when it became clear that she had gone
headlong into a passionate affection for him, he
sealed up his conscience and succumbed. He
had invented the fiction of an estranged wife ;
she pitied him, she wept for him. His life, he

had said, was at its close. She threw herself upon him, and cried out against his sentence. The narrow bonds of social convention were chains too weak to bind her. She had no fears, no doubts ; she would have no remorse. And with the lie black and stark between them they two embarked upon a hazardous new fortune.

Here in his abasement, knowing how full and irretrievable was his love for her, the man could find one plea only to abate his guilt. She had come with a reputation worn by gossip—gossip since proved foul and false ; he had regarded her only as lightly as he had thought she might ask to be regarded. But there was no hope of pardon in this ; there was no forgiveness even from himself.

He should have to tell her the story now. The terror of that necessity laid cold hands upon his heart. For four years shame had kept him from the confession. And now must he speak with the new danger of her growing coldness? She would still be tied to him, were he even now to turn the key upon his secret. The news she had broken to him that morning would link them together with stronger chains. Should he be silent the wrong he had done her and her child would lie upon his conscience only. Would it be best? He rose and paced the room. Something moved on the floor overhead; his heart wept at the sound of her. Now that the fact faced him so grimly, new currents of tenderness ran through him. He wanted her as his wife. All the bonds that society or convention or the sacred rites of religion could offer, he desired to have secured upon them both. Shame and fear must not stand between her and her justification. If he had been a coward once, he must to-day enact a newer, better part.

As he turned round in his chair, full of a sudden resolution, his glance crossed the blue-lined paper on which he had been scribbling. The uncompleted verse met his eye and solicited his attention—

'The voice of rain and wind and stream
  Foretold our summer's fall,
Forecast the breaking of the dream
  The ruined festival.
Oh, loud I heard the cold rain weep,
  The mad wind cry and call;'

He stopped, and of a sudden the verse completed itself. He seized his pen and wrote—

'But my heart's silence, dull and deep,
  Was louder than them all.'

He dropped the pen, and sat staring at the lines. Then rising, he walked across the room. The sunlight struck through the window and fell in patches on the carpet. As he went the spectre of his old sin stretched itself and preceded him, gibbering, to the door. He mounted the staircase, dully, a formless terror gnawing at his heart.

Millicent locked the door of her room and flung herself upon the bed. She wept at the indignity that was still in her thoughts; she was angry with a resentment quite passionate. But now and then a strange curiosity fluttered in her heart. She hardly knew herself for the Millicent of yesterday; she was so torn with her emotions. They came and went with the speed of pulsations. Ere this horrible revelation she had not been conscious of any change in her attitude towards Rossiter. And now, though the consciousness was thrust upon her, she did not moralise upon it; she did not even pause to inquire whether it were transient or something more fundamental. She was not a woman of that kind; she had spent all her life in little runs and gushes of impulse, taken forth-right and forgotten, times out of number.

It was in one of these reckless fits of abandonment that she had come to Rossiter; and that she had not left him was only because she had as yet felt no passion contrary to the connection. She had fallen back upon a genuine friendliness for him; it was not the mad emotion, to the delusion of which she had yielded in the first instance, but it was an affection which had worn well for five years, though it would fare ill under a strain. She did not know she had changed; at no point in her life could she have put her finger on a day in which she had awakened to the shallowness of her feeling for him. She did not realise it now. She merely lay upon the bed with all the indolence of an animal, while her consciousness was absorbed in the sensations of her mood.

Presently she arose and went to the window. Down below the streets streamed with cabs and carriages, and the sunlight dashed them with colour. Tranquilly she leaned her face against the pane and looked out. There they went, on and on incessantly, day by day, week by week. How gruesome to settle into this dead monotony! While the fools might be doing something new each day, they kept their noses to the earth and crept along between blinkers on the same old course, year in, year out. The insularity and triviality of human life were ridiculous. She wondered vaguely why she was only now finding out the tiresomeness of her existence. The thought of maternity repelled her. She winced at the approach of those unknown terrors. Her disgust was lightened by no sentiment for Rossiter. When she lost the sense of frightened anger, it was with mere inquisitiveness that she dwelt upon the future.

It was only when he had knocked twice that she opened the door to him; which done, she straightway resumed her place at the window, tapping her restless fingers on the pane. She knew why he had come; his heart was weltering in pity, and he would put his arms about her and offer consolation in soft tones. In her imagination she could see him opening his mouth, his eyes glistening with tenderness. There was something too humble and unmanly in his affection. Bah! She shrugged her shoulders with distaste.

Rossiter stood halfway to her; the poise of her head, the old familiar graces which had grown to be a part of his life, touched him with a sense of longing, even also with a sense of fear. When he spoke, the harshness of his voice made her turn round in surprise.

'Milly, we must be married,' he said.

She stared at him. 'Oh, yes' she said indifferently, after a pause, 'when it is possible.'

'It is possible now,' he replied abruptly.

'What on earth do you mean?' she asked. 'Are any more tragedies going?'

She was leaving the window and making for the arm-chair, when he took her hand in his.

'Oh, let me alone, please,' she said impatiently.

She looked into his eyes, but did not see there what she had expected. They held no pity for her, no tender light shone in them; only the shadows of fear and shame were there. He patted her hand mechanically.

'Do you remember just now that I asked you how much you could forgive?' he asked in a curious monotone. 'The time has come for me to see. I do not expect you to forgive; I only hope for you to love me still. Perhaps even that is too much. I don't know.'

She withdrew her hand, looking at him. He interested her. She sat down in the chair.

'For goodness' sake, get on,' she said. 'What has happened?'

'I want you to be married to me, to-morrow.'

'Then your wife——' she broke out. 'She is dead?'

'No,' he answered very softly. 'I have never had any wife, but you.'

The silence was broken only by the creaking of the chair. He lifted his gaze from the ground, and met hers. Before it, he quivered and winced. Two large fires flashed out and scorched into his very soul.

'You never had a wife?' she asked in a slow whisper. He made no reply. 'Let me hear what it means,' she went on in the same tense voice. 'I don't suppose I understand.'

He leaned against the foot of the bed, and held his averted face between his hands.

'I deceived you. I was a selfish coward. I did not think I loved you, and I allowed you to come to me under the supposition that I could not marry you.' She breathed very hard. 'I have nothing more to say,' he continued. 'Within the year I found out my passionate love for you, and the impossibility of telling you of my crime.'

'Why do you tell me now?' she asked.

The blood was rising in her body; it seemed to ride round and round in her head, constraining her slowly and surely to a cruel deed.

'I have told you because it has become necessary that we should be married.'

'Why?'

For the first time he looked up in astonishment. Her eyes still dwelt upon him, burning bright.

'The change—what you said just now—the child——,' he stammered.

She threw herself back in her chair, and laughed wildly and loudly.

'Is that all? My God, is that all? The mere reflection of a possible infant's possible legitimacy? You have disturbed the secret of years for that! It was quite needless, I assure you.'

All the time the thought was repeating itself in her mind, 'How can I hurt him most? What can I do or say to hurt him?' She groped about for means; she was talking at random, without a perception that her voice and words were stabbing him, feeling only that she must do and say more.

'I have no word of protest to say,' he said quietly. 'You know I love you. I only wish to know if you still can love me after this?'

'Love you!' she replied, in a deliberate voice. 'It makes no difference in my affection for you. Of course I am angry at the deception. It was, as you say, selfish and cowardly. But you have, no doubt, suffered for it. I shall get over my indignation. Oh no, there is no change in my affection.'

His eyes brightened; he straightened himself from his bowed posture, and a sigh of relief escaped him. He put out a hand to her.

'Milly, you—are—very good to me,' he said brokenly; 'I will leave you now, and to-morrow we can be married.'

'No.'

He stopped at the sharpness of his negative. She leaned forward in her chair, her elbows upon her knees, fixing him with feverish eyes. 'You had better hear my story, as I have heard yours. When I was a girl, an impulsive fool, I imagined myself into a passion for you. I left my home for the fancy, being a fool; and like a

B

fool I lived on with you for five years. This morning I discovered my mistake. I might have discovered it before if I had been given to thinking. I might have known what was the explanation of the boredom I endured, of the restlessness, of the indifferent kindliness I had for you. But I am not one who thinks ; I only feel. And when I had made one accursed discovery this morning, I made another more pleasant. It was that I am tired of you.'

He gave a cry of pain.

' I will not marry you.'

' For God's sake, Milly——' he began.

' I am not angry—I am only awake,' she said. ' You have given me the opportunity. I should have been foolishly blind enough to stay with you if you had not told me this. I am glad you did. It destroys all the ties between us.'

' But the child ? ' said Rossiter, in his whisper.

' Bah ! ' she said. ' That's the opportunity. It is that that has brought me to my senses. Though I hate it, I shall owe it a debt of gratitude.'

She regarded him triumphantly—her face glowing, her eyes bright, her bosom heaving. He stood in the centre of the room, his chin fallen upon his breast, his fingers pressing against his heart.

'I will go,' he said, in a low voice.

The door closed behind him. With a leap she was on her feet, and pacing the room with long strides of exultation. 'Free,' she said; 'free from now!' She looked out on the street, where the traffic roared, 'Free, free, free! Free to go anywhere, be any one, do anything!' The portals of her prison swung open, and the world stretched before her.

Suddenly, and in the midst of her song of triumph, she paused. A fear thrilled in her bosom. A spasm of pain, of hatred, distorted her face. With a short fierce cry, she flung herself at full length upon the bed; biting the pillows with her teeth, and clutching the blankets, she rocked to and fro.

'It shall not be,' she said. 'No; it shall not be!'

THERE was no immediate response to his knock, and, ere he rapped again, Farrell turned stupidly and took in a vision of the street. The morning sunshine streamed on Piccadilly; a snap of air shook the tree-tops in the Park; and beyond the greensward sparkled with dew. The traffic roared along the roadway, but the cabs upon the stand rode like ships at anchor on a windless ocean. Below him flowed the tide of passengers. The dispassion of that drifting scene affected him by contrast with his own warm flood of emotions; the picture—the trees, the sunlight and the roar—imprinted itself sharply upon his brain. His glance flitted among the faces, and wandered finally to the angle of the crossway, by which his cab was sauntering leisurely. With a shudder he wheeled face-about to the door, and raised the clapper. For a moment yet he stood in hesitation. The current of his

20

thoughts ran like a mill-race, and a hundred discomforting impressions flowed together. The house lay so quiet; the sunlight struck the window-panes with a lively and discordant glare. He put his hand into his pocket and withdrew a latch-key, twiddling it restlessly between his fingers. With a thrust and a twist the door would slip softly open, and he might enter unobserved. He entertained the impulse but a moment. He dared not enter in that nocturnal fashion; he would prefer admittance publicly, in the eye of all, as one with nothing to conceal, with no black shame upon him. His return should be ordinary, matter-of-fact; he would choose that Jackson should see him cool and unperturbed. In some way, too, he vaguely hoped to cajole his memory, and ensnare his willing mind into a belief that nothing unusual had happened.

He knocked with a loud clatter; feet sounded in the hall, and the door fell open. Jackson looked at him with no appearance of surprise.

'Good morning, Jackson,' he said, kicking his feet against the step. He entered, and laid his umbrella in the stand. 'Is your mistress up yet?' he asked.

'Yes, sir,' said the servant placidly; 'she's in the morning-room, sir, I think.'

There was no emotion in the man's voice; his face wore no aspect of suspicion or inquiry, and somehow Farrell felt already relieved. To-day was as yesterday, unmarked by any grave event.

'Ah!' he said, and passed down the hall. At the foot of the stairs he paused again, with a pretence of dusting something from his coat, and winced at the white gleam of his dress-shirt. Nothing stirred in the house save a maid brushing overhead, and for a while he lingered. He still shrank from encountering his wife, and there was his room for refuge until he had put on a quieter habit of mind. His clothes damned him so loudly that all the world must guess at a glance. And then again the man resumed his manliness; he would not browbeat himself for the mere knowledge of his own shame; and, passing rapidly along the hall, he pushed open the door of the morning-room.

A woman rose on his entrance, with a happy little cry.

'George!' she said. 'Dear George, I'm so glad.'

She put up her arms and lifted her face to him. Farrell shivered; the invitation repelled him; in the moment of that innocent welcome the horror of his sin rose foul before him. He touched her lightly on the cheek and withdrew a little distance.

'I'm not a nice object, Letty,' he faltered, 'see what a mess the beastly mud has made of me. And look at my fine dress-clothes.' He laughed with constraint. 'You'd think I lived in them.'

'O dearest, I was so disappointed!' said the girl. 'I sat up ever so late for you. But I was so tired. I'm always tired now. And at last I yawned myself to sleep. Wherever have you been?'

The colour flickered in Farrell's face, and his fingers trembled on the table.

'Oh, I couldn't get away from Fowler's, you know. Went there after the club, and lost my train like a fool.'

His uneasy eyes rose furtively to her face. He was invested by morbid suspicions, suspicions of her suspicion; but the girl's gaze rested frankly upon him, and she smiled pleasantly.

'That dreadful club! You shan't go there again for a week, darling. I'm so glad you've come. I was nearly being very frightened about you. I've been so lonely.' She took him by the arm. 'Poor dear, and you had to come all through London with those things on. Didn't people stare?'

'I will change them,' he said abruptly, and turned to leave.

'What!' she said archly. 'Would you go without—and I haven't seen you for so long.' She threw her arms about his neck.

'For God's sake—— No, no, Letty, don't touch me,' he broke out harshly.

The girl's lips parted, and a look of pain started into her face.

'I meant,' he explained quickly, 'I am so very dirty, dear; you'd soil your pretty frock.'

'Silly!' she returned smiling, 'and it isn't a pretty frock. I can't wear pretty frocks any longer,' she added mournfully.

He dropped his eyes before the flush that sprang into her cheeks, and left the room hurriedly.

His shame followed him about all day, dogging him like a shadow. It lurked in corners and leaped out upon him. Sometimes it crept away and hovered in the remoter distance; he had almost forgotten its attendance; and then in the thick of his laughing conversation it fell upon him black once more. It skulked ever within call, dwindled at times, grey and insignificant. When he stopped to exchange a sentence in the street, it slid away; he moved on solitary, and it ran out before him, dark and portentous. Remorse bit deep into him, remorse and a certain fear of discovery. The hours with his wife were filled with uneasy thoughts, and he would fain have variegated the cheerless monotony of his conscience by adding a guest to his dinner-table. But from this course he was deterred by delicacy; for, at his suggestion, Letty looked at him, winced a little, smiled ever so faintly, and, with an ineffable expression of tender embarrassment, drew her morning-gown closer round her body. He could not press the indignity upon her young and sensitive mind.

But the fall of night, which he had so dreaded, brought him a change of mood. The table was stocked with the fruits of a rare intelligence; the plate shone with the fine linen; and all the comforts waited upon his appetite. It was no gross content that overtook him, but the satisfaction of a body gently appeased. His sin had faded wonderfully into the distance, had grown colder, and no longer burned intolerably upon his conscience. He found himself at times regarding it with reluctant equanimity. He stared at it with the eyes of a judicial stranger. Men were so wide apart from women ; they were ruled by another code of morals. If this were a pity, it fell at least of their nature and their history. Was not this the prime lesson science had taught the world ? But still the shame flickered up before him ; he could watch its appearances more calmly, could reason and debate of it, but it was still impertinently persistent. And yet he was more certain of himself. To-morrow the discomfort would return, no doubt, but with enfeebled spirit ; he would suffer a very proper remorse for some time—perhaps a week—and then the affair would dismiss itself, and his memory would own the dirty blot no longer. As the meal went forward his temper rose. He smiled upon his wife with less diffidence ; he conversed with less effort. But strangely, as he mended, and the first horror of his guilt receded, he had a leaning to confession. Before, he had felt that pardon was impossible, but now that he was come within range of forgiving himself, he began to desire forgiveness from Letty also. The inclination was vague and formless, yet it moved him towards the subject in an aimless way. He found himself wondering, with a throb in his blood, how she would receive his admissions, and awoke with the tail of her last sentence in his ears.

'I'm so glad the servants have gone. I much prefer being alone with you, George.'

'Yes,' he murmured absently, 'they're a nuisance, aren't they?'

She pushed the claret to him, and he filled his glass abstractedly. Should he tell her now, he was thinking, and let penitence and pardon crown a terrible day? At her next words he looked up, wondering.

'Had Mr. Fowler any news of Edward?' she asked idly.

The direction of her thoughts was his; he played with the thought of confession; his mind itched to be freed of its burden.

'Oh no, we were too busy,' he laughed

uneasily. 'The fact is, you see, Letty dear—I have a confession to make——'

She regarded him inquiringly, even anxiously. He had taken the leap without his own knowledge; the words refused to frame upon his tongue. Of a sudden the impulse fled, screaming for its life, and he was brought up, breathless and scared, upon the brink of a giddy precipice.

'What confession, darling?' she asked in a voice which showed some fear.

The current of his ideas stopped in full flow; where a hundred explanations should have rushed about his brain, he could find not one poor lie for use.

'What do you mean, dearest?' said his wife, her face straightened with anxiety.

Farrell paled and flushed warm. 'Oh, nothing, my darling child,' he said with a hurried laugh; 'we played baccarat.'

'George!' she cried reproachfully. 'How could you, when you had promised?'

'I don't know,' he stumbled on feverishly. 'I was weak, I suppose, and they wanted it, and—God knows I've never done it before, since I promised, Letty,' he broke off sharply.

The girl said nothing at the moment, but sat staring at the table-cloth, and then reached out a hand and touched his tremulous fingers.

'There, there, dear boy,' she murmured soothingly, 'I won't be cross; only please, please, don't break your word again.'

'No, I won't, I won't,' muttered the man.

'I daresay it was hard, but it cost you your train, George, and you were punished by losing my society for one whole night. So there—it's all right.' She pressed the hand softly, her face glowing under the candle-light with some soft emotion.

Farrell withdrew his arm gently.

'Have some more wine, dear,' said his wife.

'She raised the bottle, and was replenishing his glass when he pushed it roughly aside.

'No more,' he said shortly, 'no more.'

The wound broke open in his conscience, red and raw. The peace which had gathered upon him lifted; he was shaken into fears and tremors, and that devilish memory, which had retired so far, came back upon him, urgent and instant, proclaiming him a coward and a scoundrel. He sat silent and disturbed, with his eyes upon the crumbs, among which his fingers were playing restlessly. Letty rose, and passed to the window.

'How dark it has fallen!' she said, peeping through the blinds, 'and the rain is pelting so hard. I'm glad I'm not out. How cold it is! Do stir the fire, dearest.'

Farrell rose, and went to the chimneypiece. He struck the poker through the crust of coal and the flames leapt forth and roared about the pieces. The heat burned in his face. There came upon him unbidden the recollection of those days, a year ago, when he and Letty had nestled side by side, watching for fortunes in the masses of that golden core. She had seen palaces and stately domes; her rich imagination culled histories from the glowing embers; while he, searching and searching in vain, had been content to receive her fancies and sit by simply with his arm about her. The thought touched him to a smile as he mused in the flood of the warmth.

Letty still stood peering out upon the street, and her voice came to him, muffled from behind the curtain.

'Oh, those poor creatures! How cold and

how wet they must be! Look, George, dear. Why don't they go indoors out of the rain?'

Farrell, the smile still upon his lips, turned his face towards her as he stooped.

'Who, child?'

'Why, those women,' said his wife pitifully, 'why don't they go home? They keep coming backwards and forwards. I've seen the same faces pass several times. And they look so bleak and wretched, with those horrid tawdry dresses. No one ought to be out to-night.'

The poker fell from Farrell's hand with a clatter upon the fender.

'Damn them!' he cried, in a fierce, harsh voice.

The girl pulled the curtain back, and looked at him.

'Darling,' she said plaintively, 'what is it? Why do you say such horrible things?'

Farrell's face was coloured with passion; he stood staring angrily at her.

'George, George,' she said, coming to him, 'why are you so angry with me? Oughtn't I to be sorry for them? I can't help it; it seems so sad. I know they're not nice people. They're dreadful, dear, of course. I've always heard that,' and she laid her face against his breast. 'But it can't be good for them to be out this wretched night, even if they are wicked.'

She pressed against him as for sympathy, but Farrell made no response. A fearful tension held his arms and body in a kind of paralysis; but presently he patted her head softly, and put her gently from him.

'I'm in a very bad temper to-night, dear,' he said slowly. 'I suppose I ought to go to bed and hide myself till I'm better.'

She clung to him still. 'Don't put me away, George. I don't mind if you are in a bad temper. I love you, dearest. Kiss me, dear, kiss me; I get so frightened now.'

A spasm contracted his features; he bent over and kissed her; then he turned away.

'I will go and read,' he said, 'I shall be better then.'

She ran after him. 'Let me come too, George. I will sit still and won't disturb you. You can't think how I hate being alone now. I can't understand it. Do let me come, for you know I must go to bed early, I was up so late last night.'

The pleading words struck him like a blow. 'Come, then,' he answered, taking her hand.

'And you may swear if you want to very much,' she whispered, laughing, as they passed through the door.

The sun rose bright and clear; the sky, purged of its vapours, shone as fine as on a midsummer day. With this complaisance of the weather, Farrell's blacker mood had passed. His weak nature, sensitive as it was to the touch of circumstances, recovered easily from their influences. Sleep had renewed the elastic qualities of his mind, and the smiling heaven set him in great spirits. Letty, too, seemed better, and ate and talked with a more natural gaiety. The nightmare of the previous evening was singularly dim and characterless. He tried to recall the terror of it, and wondered why it had so affected him, with every circumstance of happiness around—his smiling wife, a comfortable house, and the pleasant distractions of fortune. The gulf that opened between Letty and himself was there by the will of nature. He had but flung aside the conventions that concealed it. It was a horrid gap, but he had not contrived it. The sexes kept different laws, and he himself, in all likelihood, came nearer to what she would require of him than any

C

other man. He assured himself with conviction that he would forget altogether in a few days.

The day was pleasantly filled, but not too full for the elaboration of these arguments. They soothed him ; he grew philosophic ; he discussed the conditions of love with himself ; he even broached the problem in an abstract way over his coffee at the club. For the first time he thought that he had clearly determined the nature of his affection for Letty. It was integral and single ; it was built upon a pack of sentiments ; it was very tender, and it would wear extremely well ; but it was not that first high passion which he had once supposed. The unfamiliarity of that earlier exaltation had deceived him into a false definition of Love. There was none such in circulation among human bodies. There were degrees upon degrees of affection, and Letty and he stood very high in rank ; but to conceive of their love as something emanating from a superior sphere outside relation to the world and other human beings was the absurd and delightful flight of heedless passion.

He had laid his ghost, and came home to his

dinner in an excellent humour. The girl looked
forlorn and weary, but brightened a good deal
on his return. With her for audience he
chattered in quite a sparkling temper. Letty
said little, but regarded him often with great
shy eyes. He looked up sometimes to find
them upon him with a wistful, even a pleading,
gaze. She watched every movement he took
jealously. But she was obviously content, and
even gay in a sad little fashion. He did not
understand, but his spirits were too newly blithe
to dwell upon a puzzle. He noticed with scarce
a wonder little starts of pettishness which he
had never seen before. They flashed and were
gone, and the large eyes still followed him with
tenderness. She rested her arm across the
table in the middle of a story he was telling,
and rearranged his silver.

'You must not cross your knives,' she said
playfully. 'That's a bad omen.' He laughed,
and continued his narrative.

Left to himself, Farrell lit a cigarette, and
filled his glass with wine. The current of his
spirits had passed, but he felt extremely comfortable, and very shortly his mind stole after
his wife, who was playing softly in the further

room ; he could see the yellow fabric of the
distant curtains gleaming softly in the lamp-
light. He had a desire for a certain air, but
could not bring himself to interrupt. An atmosphere of content enwrapped him, and he
leaned back lazily in his chair. Reflections
came to him easily. Surely there was no
greater comfort than this serene domestic happiness, with its pleasant round of change. He
had set Letty's love and his in a place too low
for justice. It held a sweeter fragrance, it was
touched with higher light, than the commoner
affections of common people. A genial warmth
flooded his soul, and his heart nestled into the
comfort of desire. He was hot with wine, and
his whole being thrilled with the content of his
own reflections. He asked no better than this
quiet ecstasy, repeated through a suave un-
troubled life. The personal charm of that fine
body, the intimate distinctions of its subtle
grace, the flow of that soft voice, the sweet
attention of that devoted human soul—these
were his lot by fortune. They conducted him
upon a future which was strangely attractive.
He had loved her for some months more than a
year, and earlier that day he had summoned his

bridal thoughts down to a pedestrian level ; but now in this hour of sudden illumination, flushed with the kindly influence of his wine, his afternoon fancy seemed to him ungenerously clipt and tame. Letty stood for what was noble in his narrow life ; she invited him upon a high ideal way. If he were framed of grosser clay, it was she who would refine the fabric. The thought struck him sharply. He had learned to dispose his error in its proper place, among the sins, and he was not going to assign penalties unduly ; but the bare fact came home to him that he was unworthy of this woman's love, that no man deserved it. He had evilly entreated her, but he would rise to a new level in her company, and with her aid. She should renew in him the faded qualities of innocence and pure-heartedness which as a child he had once possessed. He would ask her mercy, and use her help. Her pardon should purge him of his dishonour ; she should take him to her heart, and perfect faith should rest between them.

The vision he had conceived drew his attention strongly ; he seemed to himself, and in a measure was, ennobled by this aspiration. Out of the fulness of his penitence he now desired the confession he had feared but a little time before. And, as he reflected, the notes of the piano changed, and Letty shot into a gay *chansonnette*, trilling softly over the sharp little runs. The careless leisure of the air took off his thoughts with it. It would be a bad world in which they might not be happy. The story would hurt her, he was sure; indeed, he could conjure before him the start of pain in her eyes. But after the shock she would resume her trust, and forget, as he was forgetting. He was entirely certain of her love, and, that secure, nothing could divide them. Perhaps she were better left to herself till she recovered from the blow; he would go away for a day or two. It might even take her worse than he expected, and he would have dull faces and tearful reproaches for a week or more. If this fell out, it was his punishment, and he would bear it in humility.

As his thoughts ran he had not noticed that the music ceased, and Letty's voice broke on his reverie.

'Mayn't I sit with you, dear,' she pleaded. 'It's so solitary in the big room!'

'Why, of course, sweetheart,' said Farrell

gently; 'come in, and close the door; we'll be snug for a little while in here.'

Letty stood by his chair and stroked his head.

'You never came to say good-night to me last night,' she said reproachfully.

Farrell put up his hand and took hers.

'Dearest, you must forgive me. I—I was very tired, and had a headache.'

'Ah, that was the penalty for staying up so late,' she replied playfully.

Farrell smiled and patted her hand.

'But you will come to-night, won't you?' she urged.

'Dear heart, of course I will,' he said, smiling indulgently. 'I'll come and have a long talk with you.'

. His wife sighed; in part, as it seemed, with satisfaction, and leaned her chin upon his hair.

'Life is very curious, isn't it, George?' she said meditatively, her eyes gazing in abstraction at the wall. 'There are so many things we don't know. I never dreamed——'

Farrell patted her hand again affectionately, reassuringly.

'I couldn't have guessed,' she went on

dreamily. 'It is all so strange and painful, and yet not quite painful. I wonder if you understand, George.'

'I think I do, dear,' said he softly.   ·

'Ah, but how can you quite? Girls are so ignorant. Do you think they ought to be told? I shouldn't have liked to be told, though. I should have been so afraid, but now somehow I'm not afraid—not quite.'

A note of pain trembled through her voice; she drew a sharp breath and shivered.

'George, you don't think I shall die, do you, George? O George, if I should die!'

She fell on her knees at his feet, looking into his face with searching eyes that pleaded for comfort. He drew her head towards him, a gulp in his throat, and caressed her hair.

'There, child, there!' he said soothingly, 'you are frightening yourself. Of course not, silly one, of course not.'

She crouched against his knees, and he stroked her hair tenderly. Pity pulled at his heart, and at the touch of her he was warmed with affection. He had no means of consolation save this smoothing motion of the palm, but he yearned for some deeper expression of his love and sympathy. In the silence his thoughts turned to their former occupation, and he felt nearer than ever to his wife. He would tell her when she had recovered.

She raised her head at length and looked at him.

'Oh, you will think I'm not brave,' she said tremulously, 'but I am brave—indeed, George. It is only sometimes that I get this fit of depression, and it overbears me. But it isn't me; it is something quite foreign within me: I was never a coward, dear.'

'No, darling,' he answered, 'of course you are not a coward. You're brave, very brave; you're my dear brave wife?' She smiled at him faintly. 'And you know, Letty,' he went on, still with his hand upon her head. 'I think we've been very happy together, and shall be very happy together, always. There is so much that binds us to one another. You love me, dear, don't you? and you could never doubt that I love you, could you?'

Letty shook her head. He cast down his eyes, patting the tresses softly.

'And I think you know that well enough and are certain enough of that not to misjudge me,' he resumed quietly. ' If I have made a mistake, Letty, it is not you who will be hardest on me, I am sure. It is I myself. If I have fallen into a seeming disloyalty, it is not I, as you will believe and understand, but something, as you said just now, quite foreign within me. For I could only be true and loyal and——'

He hesitated, raising his shameful eyes to her.

'What—what is it, George?' she asked anxiously, 'what have you done?' His hand rose and fell mechanically upon her head. He parted his lips with an effort, and continued. The task was harder than he had thought.

' It is right,' he said slowly, ' that we should have no secrets from one another; it is necessary, dear, that we should bear all things in common. To be man and wife, and to love each other, calls for this openness between us.' He stumbled on the threshold of his confession ; the pain of this slow progression suddenly unnerved him ; all at once he took it with a rush. ' Darling,' he cried quickly and on a sharper note, ' I want to confess something to you, and I want your forgiveness. That night I was away, I did not spend with Fowler. I spent it——'

'You spent it gambling?' she asked in a low voice.

'No,' he said with a groan, 'I spent it in another house—I spent it—I spent it in shame.'

He breathed the better for the words, even though a terrible silence reigned in the room. At least the worst part of his penalty was undergone; the explanation was over.

But when she spoke he realised, with a sense of dread, that he had not passed the ordeal.

'I don't understand, George,' she said in a voice thick with trouble; 'what is it? Where did you stay?'

The strain was too great for his weak nerves.

'For God's sake, Letty,' he broke out, 'try to understand me and forgive me. I dined too well; I was almost drunk. I left the club with Fowler very late. Oh, it's hideous to have to tell you. I met some one I had never seen since—oh! long before I loved you. I could not pass her. I—O God! can't you understand? Don't make me explain so horribly.'

The tale ran from him in short and broken sentences. His fingers twisted nervously about a wisp of her hair; his gaze had nowhere rest.

She looked full into his face with frightened eyes.

'Do you mean—those women—we saw?' she asked at last, in a voice pitched so low that he hardly heard.

'Yes,' he whispered; and then again there was silence. The agony of the suspense was intolerable. 'You will never forgive me,' he muttered.

He felt her trembling hands grow cold under his touch; and, as she still kept silence, he dropped his slow, reluctant glance to meet hers. At the sight of the terrified eyes, he put his hands towards her quickly.

'Letty, Letty,' he cried, 'for God's sake, don't look like that! Speak to me; say you forgive me. Dearest, darling, forgive me!'

She rose as if unconscious of her action, and, walking slowly to the fireplace, stood looking at the red flames.

'Letty,' he called, 'don't spurn me like this. Darling, darling!'

His attitude, as he waited for her response, there, in the centre of the room, was one of singular despair. His mouth was wried with an expression of suffering; he endured all the pangs of a sensitive nature which has been always wont to shelter itself from pain. But still she made no answer. And then she seemed suddenly taken with a great convulsion ; her body trembled and shivered ; she wheeled half-way round with a cry ; her eyes shone with pain.

'George, George!' she screamed on a horrid note of agony, and swaying for a second to and fro, fell hard across the fender and against the live bars of the grate.

Farrell sprang across the intervening space and swung her head away from the angry flames. She lay limp and still upon the hearthrug, a smear of black streaking her white arm from the elbow, the smell of her frizzled gown fusing with the odour of burned hair. Her face was set white, the mouth peaked with a spasm of pain ; the eyelids had not fully fallen, and a dreadful glimmer of light flickered from a slit in the unconscious eyes. He stood, struck weak and silent for a moment, and then flung himself upon the floor, and hung over the body.

'Letty, Letty!' he cried. 'Letty, Letty! O my God! have I killed you?' The flesh twitched upon the drawn face, and a moan issued from her lips. Farrell leapt to the bell-rope and pulled fast; and away in some distant depth the peals jingled in alarm. A servant threw open the door and rushed into the room.

'A doctor, a doctor!' cried Farrell, vehemently. 'Get a doctor at once. Your mistress is ill. Do you hear, Jackson? God, man, don't stare at me. Go, go!'

As the door closed Farrell's glance stole back to the floor. His breath came fast as he contemplated the body. It lay there as though flung by the hand of death, and wore a pitiful aspect. It forbade him; it seemed to lower at him; he could not associate it with life, still less with Letty. It owned some separate and horrible existence of itself. The flames mounting in the fire threw out great flashes upon the recumbent figure, and the very flesh took on a moving colour. Hours seemed to pass as he stood beside her, and not until the quivering eyelids denoted a return of life did he gain courage to touch her. With that she became somehow familiar again; she was no more the blank eidolon of a woman. He put his arms beneath her and slowly lifted the reviving body to the sofa. The blood renewed its course in the arteries, and she opened her eyes dully and closed them again.

The entrance of the doctor dispelled for a while the gloomy thoughts that environed him. The man was a stranger, but was welcomed as an intimate.

'She has had a shock,' said Farrell, 'you will understand. It was my doing,' he added.

The sharp change from the dreadful reveries of his solitude turned Farrell to a different creature. He was animated with action; he bustled about on errands; he ran for brandy, and his legs bore him everywhere, hardly with his knowledge. And as the examination pro-ceeded he grew strangely cheerful, watching the face of the physician and drawing inferences to his fancy. He laughed lightly at the doubt if she could be lifted to her room.

'Yes, of course,' said he.

'The stairs are steep, sir,' said Letty's maid.

He smiled, and drew back the cuffs from his strong wrists. Stooping, he picked up his wife lightly, and strode upstairs.

As the doctor was leaving, Farrell waylaid

him in the hall, and took him to the door. The
visitor drew on his gloves and spoke of the
weather; the sky threatened rain again and
the night was growing black. Farrell agreed
with him hurriedly, adding a few remarks of
no interest, as though to preserve that air of un-
concern which the doctor seemed to take for
granted; and then, with his hand on the door,
abruptly touched his subject.

'Is there any danger?' he asked.

The doctor paused and buttoned his glove.

'She is very sensitive,' said the doctor.

'It was my doing,' said Farrell, after a moment,
dropping his eyes to the floor.

'It is a dangerous time,' said the doctor.
'Very little may do damage. We can't be too
careful in these affairs.'

He finished with his gloves, and put out his
hand.

'Have I,' stammered Farrell, 'have I done
irreparable harm?'

'She is very delicate,' said the doctor.

'What will it mean?' asked the husband,
lowering his voice.

The doctor smiled and touched him with his
fingers. 'If you were to cut your finger, my

friend, a doctor would never prophesy. Events are out of all proportion to causes.' He put his own hand upon the latch. 'I will call to-morrow early,' he said, 'and will send a nurse at once.'

Farrell took his arm in a hard grip.

'Is she dying?' he asked hoarsely.

The doctor moved impatiently. 'My dear sir, certainly not,' he answered hastily. He threw open the door and emerged into the night. 'I would not distress myself with un-necessary fancies, Mr. Farrell,' said he, as he dropped down the steps.

Farrell walked down the hall to the foot of the stairs. He laid a hand upon the balustrade uncertainly. The house was engrossed in silence; then from the floor above came a sharp cry, as of a creature in pain, and a door shut softly. Trembling, he rushed into the dining-room, and hid his face in his hands. Yet that weak device was no refuge from his hideous thoughts. His brain was crowded with fears and terrors; in the solitude of that chamber he was haunted by frightful ghosts. The things stood upon the white cloth, like spectres; the lamp burned low, and splashes

D

of flame rose and fell in the ashes. He rose and poured some brandy into a glass. The muscles jumped in his hands, and the liquor spilled over the edges and stained his shirt, but the draught strung up his nerves, and brighter thoughts flowed in his mind. He pulled out a chair before the fire and sat down, meditating more quietly.

An hour later he was disturbed from his reflections by the passage of feet along the hall. His ears took in the sound with a fret of new anxiety; it portended fresh horrors to him. But in a little he realised from the voices without that the nurse had arrived, and a feeling of relief pervaded him. The footsteps passed upstairs. He sat passive within the arms of his chair and listened. A fresh hope of succour lay in those feet. The doctor and the nurse and the maid were doing what was vital; in their attentions was the promise of rescue. It was as if he himself took no part in the tragedy; he sat as a spectator in the stalls, and viewed the action only with the concern of an interested visitor. He filled another tumbler with spirit.

The alcohol fired his blood, and raised him

superior to the petty worry of his nerves. He
drank and stared in the embers and considered.
Letty was ill in a manner not uncommon; even
though it threatened the sacrifice of one life the
malady was not inevitably mortal. He had
been bidden to discharge his fears, and brandy
had discharged them for him. He turned to
fill his glass again; the fumes were in his head,
but at that moment the recollection of his last
excess flashed suddenly upon him, and, with an
inarticulate scream of rage, he dashed the bottle
to the floor, and ground the glass under his
feet. Rising irresolutely he made his way
upstairs, and paused before Letty's door. At
his knock the nurse came out and greeted him
—a strange tall woman with hard eyes.

'My wife'—he asked, 'Is Mrs. Farrell better?'

She pushed him gently away. 'I think so,'
she said; 'we shall see. The worst is over,
perhaps. You understand. Hush, she is
sleeping now at last.' He lingered still, and
she made a gesture to dismiss him, her voice
softening. 'Doctor Green will tell you best
to-morrow.'

Farrell entered his room and took off his coat.
His ears, grown delicate to the merest suspicion,

seemed to catch a sound upon the stillness, and opening the door he looked out. All was quiet; the great lamp upon the landing swung noiselessly, shedding its dim beams upon the panelled walls. He shut to the door, and once more was in the wilderness of his own thoughts.

The doctor came twice that next day. In the morning a white and anxious face met him on the stairs and scanned him eagerly.

'She is going on, going on,' said he deliberately.

'Then the danger is past?' cried Farrell, his heart beating with new vigour.

'No doctor can say that,' said the doctor slowly. 'She is as well as I expected to find her. It was very difficult.'

'But will she——' began Farrell, stammering.

'Well?' exclaimed the doctor sharply.

'Will she live?'

The doctor's eye avoided his. 'These things are never certain,' he said. 'You must hope. I know more than you, and I hope.'

'Yes, yes,' cried Farrell impatiently. 'But, my God, doctor,' he burst forth, 'will she die?'

The doctor glanced at him and then away It is possible,' he said gravely.

Farrell leaned back against the handrail and mechanically watched him pass the length of the hall and let himself out. Some one touched his arm, and he looked up.

'Come, sir, come,' said the nurse. 'You mustn't give way. Nothing has happened. She is very weak, but I've seen weaker folk pull through.'

He descended the stairs and entered the drawing-room. The room looked vacant; the inanimate furniture seemed to keep silence and stare at him; he felt every object in that place was privy to his horrible story. They regarded him sternly; he seemed to feel the hush in which they had talked together, ere he entered. He could not bear the condemnation of that silence, and sat down at the piano, softly fingering the notes. But the voices of those chords cried to him of Letty. It was her favourite instrument, the purchase of her own means, and every resonance reminded him of her. It was by her hand that melodies had been framed and fashioned from the strings; his was an alien touch. They wept for their mistress underneath his fingers; he struck at random, and melancholy cadences mourned at him. They knew his secret, too. With a horrid, miserable laugh he got up, and putting on his hat, went forth and down to his club.

The change did not distract his thoughts; the burden lay as heavy upon his mind, but at least the walk was an occupation. He came back with a bundle of letters which his indolent nature had allowed to accumulate with the porter, and, retiring to his smoking-room, made a manful effort to re-engage his attention. With this work and the hour of lunch, the time passed until the doctor's second visit. He heard the arrival, and, putting down his pen, waited in a growing fever for the sound of feet descending on the stairs. The smoking-room lay back from the hall, but Farrell flung open his door and listened. The day was falling in and the shadows were deepening about him, but still the doctor made no sign. At length he left his chair and called Jackson. The doctor had gone. He must have left without noise, and he, Jackson, had not heard him; it was the maid who had seen him go. The discovery threw Farrell into fresh agitation; his anger mingled with terror. He had wanted a report of the illness; he would have the doctor back at once; he had a thousand questions to put. Rushing up the stairs he rapped at the door of the sick-room, softly and feverishly. When the nurse presented herself he burst out impetuously. He must come in; he would see his wife; he was persistently held in ignorance of her condition, and he demanded admittance as a right. The nurse stood aside and beckoned him forward without a word. Her face was set harder than ever; she looked worn and weary.

Farrell entered softly, and with furtive fears.

'You may stay if you will be still,' said the nurse. Farrell looked at her inquiringly, beseechingly. 'No,' she added, 'you will not disturb her. She has been put to sleep. She suffered a good deal. It is a bad case.'

'Will she live?' whispered Farrell.

The nurse shook her head. 'She will not suffer much more. She will sleep. But the doctor will come in the morning. We have done everything.'

Farrell shuddered, and drew near the bed. The lamp burned low upon the dressing-table, and the chamber was in a soft twilight. He could not see her face, but her dark hair was scattered over the white pillows. A slow slight breathing filled the room. The window rattled with a passing noise. Farrell sat down upon a chair beyond the bed, and the nurse resumed her place by the fire, warming her hands. Outside the traffic passed with low and distant rumbling.

*   *   *   *   *

At the sound the nurse stole stealthily to the door and opened it.

'It is your dinner,' she whispered turning to Farrell.

He shook his head. 'I will stay here,' said he in a monotone.

'You had better go,' she urged. 'You will want it. You can do nothing.' He shook his head again impatiently. She yawned, closed the door, and, with a little sigh of weariness, retraced her steps to the hearth. Farrell rose and followed her.

'Come,' he said, bending over her, 'you are very tired. Go and rest in the next room. There is nothing to be done. I will call you. Let me watch. I wish it.' She looked at him in doubt. 'Yes, yes,' he pleaded. 'Don't you see? I must be here, and you want sleep.'

She glanced round the room, as if to assure herself that there was nothing to require her.

'Very well,' she assented, 'but call me soon;' and she vanished through the doorway like a wraith.

Farrell took his seat and regarded his wife. The breathing came gently; the masses of dark hair swarmed over the head that crouched low upon the pillow; one arm, crossing the face with shadow, lay reaching toward the brow. The room glowed with luminous gloom rather than with light. The figure rested upon its side, and the soft rise of the hip stood out from the hollows of the coverlet. In the grate the ashes stirred and clinked; the street mumbled without; but within that chamber the stillness hung heavily. Farrell seemed to hear it deepen, and the quiet air spoke louder to him, as though charged with some secret and mysterious mission. He followed the hush with a mind half vacant and wholly irrelevant. But presently the faintest rustle came with a roar upon his senses, and he sprang to his feet, stricken with sudden terror. The body moved slightly under its wrappings; the arm dropped slowly down the pillow into the darker hollows of the counterpane; the hair fell away; and the face, relapsing, softly edged into the twilight.

Farrell stood staring, mute and distracted, upon this piteous piece of poor humanity. Its contrast with the woman he had known and loved appalled him. His jaw fell open, his nails scored into his palms, his eyes bulged beneath his brows. The face rested, white and withered, among the frillings of her gown; unaccustomed lines picked out the cheeks; the mouth was drawn pitifully small and pinched with suffering. Even as he looked she seemed to his scared gaze to shrink and shrivel under pain. This was not the repose of sleep, releasing from the burden of sickness; surely he could see her face and body pricked over with starts and pangs under his eyes. It seemed to his morbid thoughts that he could read upon her moving features the horrible story of that slow disintegration. In his very sight the flesh appeared to take on the changing colours of decay. He withdrew aghast from the proximity; he blanched, and was wrung with panic. In what place within that breathing human fabric was death starting upon his dreadful round? She respired gently, the heart beat softly, the tissues, yet instinct with life, were rebuilded piece by piece. Wherein lay the secret of that fading life?

The counterpane stirred faintly, and drew his attention. His wandering glance went down the centre of that swathed body. The limbs still beat warm with blood, and yet to-morrow they must stretch out in stiff obedience to strange hands. The fancy was horrible—a cry burst from him and rang in the still and changeless chamber. The sound terrified him anew, breaking thus rudely upon the silence. He feared that she would awake, and he trembled at the prospect of her speechless eyes. And yet he had withal a passionate desire to resolve her from this deathly calm, and to see her once more regarding him with love. She hung still upon the verge of that great darkness, and one short call would bring her sharply back. He had but to bend to her ears and whisper loudly, and that hovering spirit would return. He stood, a coward, by the bed.

And now the lips in that shrunken face parted suddenly, the bosom quickened, and the throat rattled with noises. It flashed upon him that this at last was the article of death, and

vainly he strove to call for help; his voice
stifled in his mouth. She should not so dissolve
at least; she should breathe freely; he would
give her air—and, springing with an effort to
the window, he flung it back. The cool air
flowed in, and, turning quickly, he looked down
upon the bed.

The eyes had fallen open, and were set upon
him, full and wide. Unnerved already as he
was, the change paralysed him, and he stood
for a moment stark and motionless. The fire
flared up and lit the face with colour; the eyes
shone brightly, and he seemed to see into their
deepest corners. There was that in them
from which he recoiled at length slowly and
with horror. They fastened upon him mutely,
pleading with him for mercy. They were like
the eyes of a creature hunted beyond a prospect
of defence. Dumbly they dwelt on him, as
though in his presence they had surrendered
their last hope. They seemed to wait upon him,
submissive to their fate, yet luminous with that
despair. He tried to speak, but the wheels of
his being were without his present rule, and he
might only stand and shudder and give back
glance for glance. He looked away, but his

fascinated gaze returned again to those re-
proaching eyes. They did not waver; it was
as if they dared not lose their sight of a pitiless
enemy. They recognised him as their butcher.
Even through her sleep this poor weary
soul had come to understand his proximity,
and had woke up, in fright at his unseemly
neighbourhood.

The lamp sputtered, a tongue of flame shot
up the chimney, and the rank smell of smoke
stole through the room. Farrell retreated to
the table, and dressed the wick with trembling
fingers. The act relieved the strain, but when
he turned the eyes were watching still. They
bereaved him of his powers, and under the spell
of their strange and horrible attraction he
sweated in cold beads. They burned upon him
from the distance, two great hollows of light,
like shining stars, holding that awful look of
wistful fear. There was no room in his mind
for any sensation save the one; he could not
think; he had no reckoning of the time his
agony endured. But outside, at last, the bell of
a clock-tower boomed far away and some hour
was struck. And suddenly it seemed to him
that the lustre of those great eyes grew dimmer;

the look of sad expectation died slowly away. They stared with a kinder light. It was his fancy, perhaps, but at least it seemed that no strange creature now regarded him with unfamiliar terror, but his own dear Letty watched him again with soft affectionate eyes. His limbs grew laxer under him ; and, with a little sob of relief, he stole forward, an uncertain smile of greeting growing round his mouth.

'Letty,' he whispered, 'my darling, are you better ?'

He drew near the bed, and put out his arm eagerly and gently ; but in an instant a start rose quickly in her face, the eyes kindled with a horrible look of panic, and with a faint repulsive gesture of the hands she shrank deeper into the wrappings. A little sigh followed : the limbs fell slowly back, and the eyes, with their dreadful terror, stared vacantly into Farrell's ghastly face.

The coverlet went on rustling as the bed-clothes settled down.

MR. ATKINSON

WHEN she looked round again the young man was still staring at her. She watched him furtively, and though at intervals his attention wandered to the stage, it strayed back to her with a persistence that set her heart beating under the vain little bodice. She felt his admiration to be distressing, but there was nothing impudent in the stare, and tiny thrills of satisfaction played throughout her body. Between the turns she heard Jack talking in jerks of conversation, but with that eloquent tribute to her charms at hand, her mind was too vagrant for more than fragmentary intelligence. He was very superior, she reflected, quite the gentleman in quality; his moustache betrayed a fine acquaintance with the world; and still he had the wit to adore with discretion and a proper feeling of respect. Her obvious distraction at last drew Jack's attention.

'What yer looking at?' he asked. 'Ain't he turned out, too? Reach-my-downs at five bob!'

Chuckling, he turned to join in the welcome of a popular dancer. Laura made no answer; but, as the young man's eyes were now upon the performer, regarded his dress with more care. The gibe dropped pointless; he had beyond doubt the air of distinction, and his clothes were 'bespoke' to the most indolent observation. Jack's wit was rough of edge, and, though it was as a rule the gift for which she most admired him, it jarred now upon her taste. She retired from mental touch with him, and grew dreamful in her isolation. She watched a shadow in the corner of her eyes, and from it learned the movements of the stranger. She would have liked to meet his gaze, but shrank from the audacity with the diffidence of her conscious admiration.

The serio sent Jack choking into laughter, and he was fain to share his amusement with her.

'Did y' hear that?' he asked. 'Wasn't it good? We'll have him again. Didn't you hear?'

Laura grimaced with some disdain. 'I thought

it was rather vulgar,' said she, and concealed as
it were, in the thick of the applause, sent a shy
glance at her admirer by the pillar.

'That chap's had about enough o' standing,
strikes me,' remarked Jack, following her gaze.
'Wants to show hisself off as a swell.'

In the lull that succeeded the exit of the
favourite he professed an intolerable thirst, and
forthwith made for a distant bar. Scarce conscious of his departure Laura held her eyes a
moment full upon the young man, who left his
pillar and lounged along the promenade towards
her. A thrill took her at the heart, but she contemplated the footlights with a fixed vision.
Something dropped into an empty seat beside
her; she turned with a self-conscious start, and
found the stranger looking at her. He raised
his hat and took the cigar from his mouth.

'Pretty 'ot here, Miss?' he said. 'Wouldn't
you like some refreshment?'

'He's gone for some,' said Laura in a flutter.
The young man made no immediate reply, but
after a pause remarked—

'I spotted you soon as ever you come in.'

Laura smiled timidly and shifted her bangle
about her wrist.

E

'It's a nice programme, ain't it?' she said.

'I dunno now,' responded the stranger with a note of sadness. 'I haven't heard much, I've been too busy ever since you come in.' He halted, while Laura tried to direct her attention upon the stage. 'That ain't your brother?' said the young man hopefully.

'No, only a friend,' returned Laura with a show of hesitation.

'I suppose I shan't see you again?' said the stranger gloomily.

Laura had nothing to answer. At this moment she was aware that some one was pushing hastily past the occupants of the seats upon her left, and of a sudden Jack stood before her.

'Come on,' he said curtly, 'let's get out of this.'

She rose obediently and followed him, but as she passed the intruder some shaft from his eyes made her pause. She put out her hand.

'Good-bye,' she said, and gave a little laugh.

Withdrawn from the neighbourhood of the stranger Jack stopped.

'What did you talk to him for?' he asked in a tone of annoyance.

'I didn't ; he talked to me,' was her answer.

'Thinks a lot of hisself,' he went on, 'but he ain't going to insult my girl—fat-head !'

Laura was filled with indignation at his conduct, but the excitement of the incident had thrown her at his mercy, and had rendered her incapable of original action. She was too stirred by the occasion to express her feelings in sulks ; she took a seat at his dictation, and tried to resume her interest in the programme. She would have liked to peer into the crowd for the disconsolate stranger, but was forbidden by her own visible emotions ; and it was by a pure accident that she espied him drinking at the bar almost within hand-reach of her dainty skirts. Jack, too, had noticed this proximity, and she glanced at him fearfully. He made a step as though to address the obnoxious young man, but suddenly turned and took Laura's arm.

'I'm off out of this,' he said. 'Come along.'

She made no protest ; her feelings were too strong for words. She left with her sweetheart, but, as they issued by the doors, could not refrain a glance behind her. It was so precipitate that she got only a confused sense of

the audience, and the next instant they were
in the street. Jack went at a rush, an angry
colour in his face.

'I believe you meant encouraging him!' he
said. She answered nothing, and he broke out
rudely. 'Don't you see, he wanted you to give
yourself away, you fool!'

In the cool air, and removed from the embarrassment of a public audience, she was able
to steady her indignation into words.

'I'll trouble you not to call me a fool, Jack
Atki'son,' said she; 'and if you'll please leave
go of my arm I'll be obliged.'

'Got the hump now, I s'pose,' he replied.

For answer she wrenched her arm from him
and walked on in silence. Jack moved by her
side uncomfortably. Now that the incentive
of his jealousy was gone he was returning to
his normal mood of affectionate good-nature,
and was disturbed by his sweetheart's anger.
Once or twice he made an effort to catch her
hand as she swung along, but each time was
repulsed, and retreated with an awkward sense
of shame.

'Look here, Laura,' he said at last. 'This
ain't going on, is it? You don't mean to make

anything out of this?   I didn't mean any harm
—straight, I didn't.'

'You're a nice sort of chap to come out with,'
was her reply.   'No one's to look at a girl, or
it's as good as an insult.   Think I can't take
care of myself, I s'pose?   Think I dunno what's
proper for a lady?'

'Well,' said Jack, a sense of injury mounting
at this rebuff, 'and I know what's proper conduct for a gentleman—so there.'

There seemed nothing more to be said, and
without further conversation they accomplished
their journey. At the shop door, Laura rang
with an irritated jerk.   She had not offered
him her lips, and he stood irresolutely on the
pavement.

'I s'pose you're going on?' she said indifferently.

'Yes, it ain't my practice to force my welcome,' was his moody answer.

With a curt good-night Laura closed the
door, and he strode angrily down the street.
A moment after, it stole softly open and she
was looking into the darkness.   Jack's footsteps were sounding on the flags, and a lamp
flickered unsteadily across the way.

As she shut the door again she caught sight of a blacker shadow clinging beneath the cover of the gaslight. Something jumped into her heart; she ran upstairs, and entering her room threw open the window. The breath of the night touched her hot cheeks, and over the road fanned the gas aslant into a flare. The shadow leaning against the post started into sudden life under the blaze, and took off its hat.

Laura closed the window with a start, and sat down on her bed quickly. She had come in with a sullen sense of annoyance, but had no desire to discuss Jack with herself. Outside stood that shadow watching her window, and in her thoughts was no room save for the magic of this devotion. She tingled with such sensations as she had not felt since Jack had suddenly put his arm round her waist some six months before; and in the resumption of this forgotten and exulting thrill she fell asleep—triumphant.

On his passage to his work next morning, Jack, as was his custom, halted before the grocer's shop to whistle his early serenade. No signal answered his devout performance, at which he repeated the air with misgivings. Thereupon a face appeared at the window on

the second floor, and a white frilled arm, thrust
through the aperture, waved at him a handkerchief. She had been wont to kiss her
fingers to his salutation, and, as he reflected
upon the change, his head sank sulkily on his
shoulders, and he slouched along the street at
a furious pace. All day was he held from sight
of her, and the quarrel lay heavy on his heart;
but in the evening he went round to the shop
to patch at once that horrible breach. Laura
met him pleasantly, and suffered his embrace
without remonstrance.

Neither made any reference to the misunder-
standing of the previous night; it seemed that
it had dropped into oblivion in this renewal of
their love. The shadow had been too im-
material, too visionary; her fancy stirred and
settled; for this substantial, measurable devotion the flimsy fabric of her dream was too
poor an exchange.

For the next few days Laura did not fail at
the window with her morning greeting; and
Jack, wholly recovered from his fears, had
fallen back upon his old temper of facetious
affection. But one evening, within a week of
the untoward incident, he called unexpectedly

upon his sweetheart, and entering the small parlour with some precipitancy, stopped aghast in the doorway; for there, in the laughing company of Laura and her mother, was the obnoxious stranger of the music-hall. In the thick of some jest he ceased, and met Jack's eyes uneasily; but Laura started alertly to her feet. Her eyes sparkled, her cheeks flushed red; she was plainly under some unusual excitement. For a moment she stammered with an access of confusion, but recovering, ran on gaily.

'O Jack,' said she, 'you did rush us! We've been laughing fit to split. This is a friend of mine, Mr. Atki'son—Mr. Field.'

'Go along, sit down, Jack,' said Laura's mother.

Jack took a seat in silence, fixing his eyes on the vacant wall.

'You was telling us'—began Laura's mother.

'P'raps Mr. Atki'son has heard it,' said the stranger politely.

'Oh no, he ain't,' returned the mother.

Jack made no response, and she pushed jocularly at his shoulder, 'Where've you left your tongue?' she inquired.

'Leave him alone. It ain't his day out. You go on, Mr. Field,' said Laura, bending her shining eyes upon the young man.

Mr. Field resumed his narrative, which was broken at points by the women's laughter, while Jack sat staring blankly at the wall. About him the talk grew livelier, but though every word and action of the party burned into his jealous soul, he was at the elaborate pretence of hearing nothing.

'What sulks you've got!' remarked Laura's mother.

Laura herself was in gay spirits, and to all outward showing free of embarrassment. She was not in the habit of closely inspecting her feelings, and the delicacy of the situation escaped her notice. She joined her mother in rallying her sweetheart upon the temper he was displaying.

'Oh, this is stupid behavin',' said she impatiently. 'Why don't you talk, Jack? It's my go to-day.'

'Seems to me,' said Mr. Atkinson, sullenly, 'there's been enough of talking. I can't gab all day like some people.'

'Hark at him,' said the mother, laughing.

'Ain't he in a bad temper? That's one for you, Mr. Field.'

Jack's mouth relaxed; he had a vague sense that he had discomfited his rival, and the thought improved his mood. His eyes wandered all over the stranger contemptuously, and rested on his patent leather boots.

'You oughter wear them, Jack,' said the mother, placidly, noticing his gaze.

'Pooh!' returned he, and looked at Laura.

'Well, haven't you got something what you can tell us?' she asked.

Jack mumbled inaudibly.

'What say?' said Laura.

Jack got upon his feet.

'Look here, I'm going off,' he said brusquely. 'I've got some one waiting for me, and I can't afford to hang on any longer.'

'You go on,' said Laura's mother, staring at him with amiable laughter.

Jack set his eyes on Laura, who said nothing. He took a step to the door, but even in his sore irritation the strain of so cold a departure was too severe for his discipline. He turned and went up to her.

'Good-night,' he said, and endeavoured to draw her to him.

'Leave go, Jack,' said she, withdrawing from the menace of a kiss, 'don't be stupid. You do fool me. I was just all to rights. Leave go, I say.'

She snapped away her hands with some asperity, and made a show of smoothing her dress. Mr. Field looked on with embarrassed eyes, and the mother was back in her chair shaking with merriment. Jack left the room quickly.

The window was shuttered close and vacant as he went by next morning, and the jealous anger hardened upon him; he made no call at the house that evening, according to his unbroken habit since their engagement. But upon the second day of this abstinence love wore his pride into rags, and he plaintively betook himself to the little shop. Laura's mother was serving a customer across the counter, and greeted him with affable indifference. He stopped.

'Where'd Laura pick up that fellow?' he asked bluffly.

'That you?' inquired the woman. 'I dunno,

Jack. He come in to buy something, and she seen him and reco'nised him.'

Jack snorted.

'He's a polite chap—quite the gentleman,' went on the mother. 'Why didn't you come in last night?'

'Did he come?' asked Jack.

'Yes. He come to ask us to go to the 'all. He's in the linen-drapery,' said Laura's mother irrelevantly.

Jack pushed through the shop and went into the parlour. Laura, at her ease on the sofa, was reading the *Family Herald*, and flashed upon him after his long absence with so sudden a charm that his heart melted within him. He went up and threw his arm round her. Laura struggled.

'Don't!' said she crossly, and pushed him away.

Cowed and dejected, he stood in the middle of the room, while she continued her reading with an ostentatious air of inattention.

'I say,' he said at last; 'come and see the Brothers German, Laura.'

She shook her head, her eyes still upon her page.

'I ain't got time,' she replied.

'You've got time to go with that fool of a linen-draping chap,' retorted Jack furiously.

Laura started.

'Who told you I was going with him?' she asked.

'Your mother did,' was his answer.

'She don't know anything about it,' said Laura with embarrassed dignity.

Jack made no answer; he was kicking the leg of the sofa viciously. His blood ran fiercely, but he did not clearly see his way to any retort or action. Under feint of absorption she watched him anxiously out of the narrows of her eyes.

'You won't come?' he said at length.

'I got too much to do,' she answered; and added presently, 'I'll go another night.'

He went out and slammed the door with an oath.

Events marched rapidly for them both. Though he paid no visit to the grocer's shop during the next few days, Jack hung about the neighbourhood from the fall of evening, and once or twice he saw the linen-draper enter by the door of which he had once had the liberty. All day the jealous thought pursued him at his work, and at night entered into his soul and gnawed upon it. He dashed home at midnight embittered and reckless. Hour after hour he sat in the public-house across the way, drinking himself into a dull and vacant animal, and watching the light in her bedroom window. He wrote a letter in terms of the wildest love and indignation, to which no answer was vouchsafed. Some two nights later, as he kept his faithful guard, flushed and agog with whisky, he saw the door open over the way, and Laura and his rival passed into the street. He rose and went out. They walked towards the main thoroughfare that ran at the bottom of the road, and he stole after them. Upon their track he followed into the thick of the town, and entered behind them at the doors of a music-hall.

From the promenade he watched them with the eyes of a lynx. No expression of their features, no turn of their heads, escaped his jealous gaze. He drank at the bar and spied upon them still. Their relations seemed intimate ; she giggled · and nudged him, he looked affectionately upon her ; she tapped his check with her programme; he insinuated his arm behind her seat. The wretched creature could refrain no further; the spirit clouded his remaining senses; the arteries beat in his forehead. He pushed swiftly forward, white with rage, and emptied his glass in the face of the linen-draper. The victim spluttered and jumped to his feet and Laura gave a little shriek—but on the one instant Jack was in the hands of a tall policeman and the next was panting hatless in the drizzle without.

'What a coward!' said Laura with trepidation, and earnestly scanning the face of her companion for traces of the injury. 'Did he hurt you?'

'No,' said the linen-draper complacently. 'It ain't much. Spoilt my collar and tie though, dirty beast!'

'Brute!' assented Laura.

'Look here,' said Mr. Field, who had seen in this accident a divine opportunity. 'What d'you say? Now's the time to tell him it's off—see?'

Laura looked anxious.

'You never liked him, you know,' he explained.

'No,' said Laura taking courage, 'only him and me kept company. I didn't know anything then. You ain't responsible for that, are you?'

'No, might as well be for all you do when you're a kid,' answered Mr. Field. 'You write him a letter to-night.'

Laura made no answer; he took hold of her hands, and she met his look with a smile.

Jack crept home miserably. His passion had flown out in that one pitiful exhibition, and his mind had come to a stage of decrepitude. He threw himself upon his bed, damp and dishevelled. Giddy with the spirit he had taken, his head went round and round, and when he closed his eyes he had a sick sensation of falling in space. His mind declined to fix itself; no definite impression did he get from his thoughts. The linen-draper, Laura, the policeman who had thrust him forth, swam in his brain together. He realised that he had been ousted from the affections of his sweetheart, but the fact conveyed no meaning to him, touched upon no emotion. A carcass of vague thoughts, he lay and let the hours go by, until at length he fell asleep from the sheer fatigue of his rude passions.

But in the morning his misery came back to him, active, unappeased. Indeed, almost ere he definitely awoke rifts opened in the vacancy of his brain through which his trouble lowered upon him. He had the intermittent sense of a horror somewhere close and imminent. When he arose he looked out of his window upon a smiling street; the sun shone brightly, and the primroses in the window-sill across the way blew softly in the morning air. He was abandoned by this jocund world, and might only sit and watch it from afar. A pain stirred dully in his heart, and when he thought upon his rejection, cut into him with a sharp point. Mechanically he took his breakfast, and departed to his work, a chaos of distractions. Nothing fell into its proper place in his mind; the rude street cries and noises of the traffic touched him on the raw; at each interruption upon the dizzy course of his brain he would start—the intrusion grew for a moment into monstrous significance, the one fact in his environment; and then the fluttered imagination sank and fell, and the ceaseless round was resumed. As he performed his duties at the counter, one of his fellows chaffed him upon his melancholy.

F

'I've 'ad a bad time,' he answered listlessly.
'This world ain't all skittles. I dunno but what
I'd like to do for myself.'

The circling anguish—for it was nothing
more definite than that—deadened his brain
and left him stupid over his work; and at
midday without warning he vanished and made
his way home. For hours he lay upon his bed,
silent and consumed with pain, until the sun
fell over the city and the grey twilight diffused
about the streets. At last in his heart there
rose suddenly a flood of pity for himself, and
he burst into tears. The pain had grown so
taut that in the end it had snapped, and he
looked out on the shouting road with eyes that
saw now and ears that heard. The soft air
brushed his face, and with wet eyes he hummed
a pathetic ditty of the halls. *Wait till the
clouds roll by, Jennie*, rang in his hearing most
melancholy, with a peculiar gratification. He
sang it through persistently, over and over
again, crooning the refrain with sad gusto.
By and by, as the lights started up in the
lamps, a voice hailed him from the pavement.

'Chi-yike!' it called, 'Chi-yike!'

He looked down upon a chum with whom

he had been wont to undertake many jovial adventures. He shook his head at the beckoning finger.

'I ain't coming out,' he said; and, swelling with a miserable pride, 'I'm smashed up, Jim,' he added. 'Don't you be surprised what yer 'ear of me.'

'You are a crock!' commented the friend, and then as Jack made no movement to descend, 'So long!' he added and slipped off, whistling.

Jack sang on drearily. All the sentimental songs in his repertory were called to his service. One after the other he crooned them in the growing darkness, and when he had exhausted his list he began it again. He had no doubt, now that he could think, that his was the most tragic fate in the world, and that this music was his swan song, wherein his passion and his love were for the last time expressed.

At nine a letter was pushed beneath the door. At a glance he saw it was from Laura, but so extreme a stage had he reached in his self-commiseration that, so far from clutching at a last hope, he had even a desire that the communication should consort with his gloom. Indeed, it was so; for the letter had been inspired by his rival the linen-draper, and rounded the tragedy to a conclusion.

'After such behaviour as last night,' she wrote in her sprawling characters, 'you won't be surprised at me breaking it off.'

No, he was not surprised; he was even conscious of a trivial gladness that the reverse should be so complete. His blood ran sentimentally; he could indulge at once his love and his supreme misery. His passion could meet no return from Laura, but at least he had the right of neighbourhood, the privilege of possession. He had no animosity in his heart against her; he had not even an active feeling of jealousy for his supplanter. But he should like to be near her—with her pretty ways, her lovely hair, the manifold attractions upon the memory of which he lingered at this moment.

The melancholy ditties reminded him of his final part in the drama, and as he breathed them softly he could see her in the little parlour, alert, so sweet, listening for a footstep. The handle turned at the door, and the linen-draper entered. She flew to meet him; Jack's plaintive murmur ceased suddenly. He rose, took from

the mantelpiece his cheap revolver, and went
out.

*　　*　　*　　*　　*

Laura's mother looked up in mild astonishment as he entered the shop.

'Well, you are a stranger, Jack,' she said;
''bout time you did make it up, I should say.'

He passed through with a mechanical salutation, and entered the house beyond.   Laura sat
alone in the parlour as he had pictured her in
his thought.   When he entered she started to
her feet, coloured, and sat down again.

' I got your letter,' he said quietly enough.

' I wonder you come,' she answered without
looking at him.

' You 've taken him on ? ' he asked.

She made no answer.   His eyes glittered and
his pulse throbbed heavily.

' S'pose you think you 've done better,' he
said.

' You ain't a gentleman, or you wouldn't
come here after all what I said,' she answered.

He was drinking in all her actions with
perfervid gaze.   She looked so sweet and fresh,
and she had now passed into the hands of his
rival.   She rose and made for the door.

' If you ain't going, I am,' she said shortly.

He put out a hand and stopped her.

'You leave me be, Mr. Atki'son,' she cried indignantly. 'Don't you touch me now.'

For answer he pulled her to him quickly, and drew his revolver from his pocket. In her struggle she saw the weapon and gave a sharp scream. A fierce pulse of exultation thrilled through him ; he put the barrel to her forehead and pulled the trigger. Her fingers fastened convulsively on his arm, and, ere the report died away, it was followed by another. The sounds brought Laura's mother to the door, her face white, her eyes bulging from her head. Motionless, she stared fearfully at the two bodies.

THE EDGE OF THE PRECIPICE

GALWORTHY threw open the window and looked down. The street was very still and dark, but a black patch of deeper shadow filled the doorway.

'Who is it?' he called. 'Is it Moreton?'

'Please let me in,' said a voice from below. It rang tremulously in the quietude, and his pulse quickened at the recognition.

'Why,' he said, 'it is—surely——'

'It is Betty Verinder. Oh, be quick, be quick!'

He sprang from the window, and, flinging back his door, ran down the stairs precipitately. A woman stepped out of the portico into the twilight of the hall.

'You are astonished,' she said, with a little laugh. 'No wonder. How late is it? Never mind. Take me upstairs.'

'Nothing has happened?' he asked eagerly. 'There is no one ill?'

'Oh, let us go upstairs! No,' she gasped impatiently; 'I've come on a midnight adventure. Don't you ever?'

A queer sense of elation possessed him as he led the way to his rooms, but he could not have determined whether it was wholly pleasant or in part compounded of pain. The girl flung herself excitedly upon a sofa. She put her hands over her eyes, and the cloak slipped from her shoulders, leaving bare her soft white neck and arms. His brain whirled at the sudden apparition, and for a time he merely looked at her, speechless.

'Why don't you ask why I have come?' she said at length from between her fingers; and then, tossing back her head, she faced him boldly, as it were resolutely, a spot of scarlet burning in either cheek. 'Don't you think it very bad and mad? I'm sure you do. But I—I think I was made to break all laws—all, every one of them—Commandments and all.' And she leaned back deeper into the sofa.

'I'm very glad to see you, Miss Verinder,' said Galworthy, contriving at last to recall his wits. 'It was a happy thought of yours to call and cheer my loneliness.'

His words were stupidly conventional, but he could not take his eyes from her, and she winced before him.

'Yes,' she replied, and ran on impetuous: 'I was at the Ormerods. You know them. Bessie's a silly girl, but I'm fond of her. She took too much champagne to-night. I didn't, though you might think it.'

'I didn't think it at all,' he stammered, 'I assure you.'

He met her glance, and she seemed as though she would have spoken, but forbore. She shifted uneasily; her feet stirred incessantly beneath her dress. He had always particularly admired her eyes, so large and full of light; and now they looked upon him, he fancied, with dumb and private entreaties. What they would have said he could not have phrased: he was but conscious that they pleaded with him. She rose with a little shiver, and went forward to the fireplace.

'Mr. Galworthy, may I just look in your glass?' she said. 'I hope my hair is more or less orderly. Oh, how dreadful!'

He turned away with a quick instinct of intelligence, and fumbled among his books.

The girl stared mutely at her own reflection in the mirror; she parted her lips and sighed; she pushed her hair back from her high forehead. Her breath came easier; she patted her cheeks softly, and drew her fingers across her weary eyelids. Then she resumed her seat, and at the sound of her voice he came forward.

'I want you to come and dine with us on Friday,' she began; 'my mother is very anxious that you should, and you have never come to see us for ages. I wonder why?'

Her voice was calm and deliberate; her face subdued into an appearance of quiet interest; her whole aspect breathed now of serene self-possession.

He stammered a little in his reply—

'I should be delighted. Your mother is very kind. Yes; it's a long time since I saw you.'

'How long have you known me?' she asked abruptly.

'I think it's a year.'

'Yes, a year. You don't know me very well, or you wouldn't have been surprised at seeing me. I don't like my friends to leave me, and I thought I would take you by storm. I did.'

He laughed softly, reassured by her self-possession. After all, it was not so wonderful, but it was very pleasant.

'And now,' said he gaily, 'do let me offer you some refreshments.'

'Refreshments!' she cried, throwing up her hands. 'Have I not dined, and in state? And have we not had champagnes and wines innumerable?' She looked at him quizzically; then she stopped suddenly, and her smile died away. 'Yes; perhaps I might. I've not really had much champagne, though you mayn't believe me—not nearly so much as the Fenton girls.' And she tittered with a return of her former embarrassment.

He poured her out a glass of wine; but he did not see her hand tremble as she took it.

'The Fenton girls were bold and noisy,' she resumed. 'You should have heard them. I know my own reputation pretty well, I think: Society is a kind of whispering-gallery. But, my dear Mr. Galworthy, Betty Verinder retreated from the field to-night, buying an ignoble peace by surrender. Lady Wilmot simpered and stuck in the palate for all the world like a stale sweetmeat. She wears the airs of a rose blowing in a wilderness. Reputations went up in smoke with the cigarettes, and Kitty's favourite Canon was distracted between her sentimental eyes and prayers for the company.'

Galworthy laughed oddly. He had not known her long, and she was given to shocking him. He took her for a most audacious wit, with the talk of the town in her ears. She ceased, and rose unexpectedly from her seat.

' I must go,' she said hurriedly. ' I don't know what possessed me to come in.'

' Please don't,' he urged. ' At any rate, finish your wine.'

She met his look for a moment, and sank slowly back into the chair. An unusual sparkle animated his sober eyes ; his colour had quickened as he spoke. For a moment she said nothing, and then—

'Why have you not been to see us ?' she asked.

He put his arm upon the mantelpiece and looked into the empty grate.

' Has it been long ? ' he inquired.

' Ages,' she returned, and encountered his eyes once more. The sparkle spread into broader waves of light.

'I'm sorry, but I——'

'Why didn't you come last week when we asked you?'

'I was afraid,' he said simply.

'Afraid!' she echoed, with a feint of levity. 'Afraid! and of what?'

It was as though she had put the question without the expectation of a reply, and indeed with but partial consciousness of her own words. But he answered, shading his eyes with his hand—

'Afraid of meeting you again, afraid of caring for you too much.'

He spoke in low tones; and she answered in tones as low, her eyes fluttering over the patch of carpet towards which she had bent her head—

'Why not?' she asked.

'There are so many others. I haven't much opinion of myself. I know how stupid I am. Who am I to have any confidence? I was afraid, Miss Verinder.'

A spasm contracted her shoulders, as if she had felt a sudden chill. She bent her head still lower.

'You needn't have been afraid,' she said.

With a quick movement he took her hand, and she felt his fingers trembling.

'Please look at me,' he whispered ; 'please look at me.   I don't understand.'

She raised her face.   Passion and entreaty leaped forth from his deep-lit eyes upon her ; to him hers were as a sky of stars.   He stooped upon his knees.

'May I kiss you?' he asked brokenly.   She winced, moved her foot restlessly upon the carpet, and sighed.

'Yes,' she replied abruptly.

'Dearest,' he said softly, caressing her.   'It was some kind god surely that sent you here to-night.'   She laughed, and in her laugh rang a note of harshness.

'Perhaps it was only the champagne,' she said.

'Hush!   You mustn't say that.   You make yourself out so bad, and I know you better.'

In his speech he was as awkward as in his actions.   He put out a clumsy hand as though to touch her again, but she drew back uncertainly.

'Do you think you really do?' she asked, with a suspicion of weary scorn in her voice. 'How wonderfully you men read women!'

'Don't make fun of me,' he pleaded. 'Just after you have given me the greatest and most unexpected happiness in life, don't let a false note be struck.'

She made no immediate answer, but suffered him to take and kiss her hand.

'I think you have probably made a mistake,' she said slowly. 'You are so young.'

'I am as old as you, dear.'

'We don't look at life from the same corner.'

'All the better for us,' he retorted cheerfully.

'You don't understand me.'

'I love you.'

She smiled and regarded him pitifully; he bent forward and kissed her full upon the lips. She covered her face with her hands and shook with little sobs of emotion.

'Are we really going to be married, then?' she asked. 'Shall we be married to-morrow? Next week? When? Oh, let us be married —yes, and be done with misgivings! Hush! What's that?' She broke off in the midst of the hysterical sentences, and, starting to her feet, listened, her face pale and rigid.

'It's only a cab passing, dear.'

'Has it passed? Listen!'

They waited, erect and silent, until the wheels rattled into the distance. Then she turned to him quickly.

'Let me go now,' she said breathlessly.

'Please——' he urged. 'It's not late. Just five minutes more, and then I'll put you into a cab.'

She yielded slowly to the gentle pressure of his hands, and declined into a chair, where she sat very still, her eyes fastened upon the floor. A little timorously he stroked her hair, as though he were not sure yet of his liberties. Indeed, it might have seemed so, for presently she stirred and pushed his hand from her head.

'What is the time?' she asked feverishly.

'It wants still ten minutes to twelve,' said Galworthy. 'But you're not going yet?'

A tiny sigh of relief escaped her. She moistened her lips and looked him square in the face.

'Do you think you're quite in earnest?' she asked. 'And do you love me as much as you seem to?'

He made an eager protest which fell harmlessly before her dispassionate calm. It was, he could not help thinking, as though she sat and judged him upon some quite remote and impersonal matter.

'We have nothing in common,' she said sadly. 'It would be a great disappointment. We should come to hate each other.'

'No!' he said hotly.

'I have both temper and talent,' she continued. 'I will be frank. You have neither. The world amuses me; save for your books and pictures, it bores you. You would never have the bad taste to take an interest in life. You are a dilettante; I am of the profession of livers. Anything great, an indignity, a sudden blow, a sharp surprise, would turn your interests sour for you; me it would leave untouched. You lack vitality as a wraith in your own dreams. I have no remorse, and you have a sensitive conscience.'

'What does all this mean, darling?' said Galworthy with an astonished little laugh. 'What nonsense you talk! We love each other.'

'I have every impudence in the world; and you are a stack of modesties,' she pursued. 'I should be a bitter grief to you.' She rose and laid her trembling fingers on the mantel-

G

piece, as though for support. 'I think within the year,' she said slowly, 'we should find each other out.'

'My dearest——' he began.

She put her arm on his shoulder laughing.

'Do you love me so much? Would you marry me to-morrow?' she asked impetuously.

'Yes, *yes*!' he cried, kissing her.

She put back her head and laughed, and the laugh rang through the room like the tinkling of a sweet bell.

'"Yes, yes," you say,' she cried. 'The phantom has clothed himself in flesh and blood. "Yes, yes." And yet I'm sure I should get to hate you. Oh, what a pity! I'm afraid we've been talking fearful nonsense. We could never marry. Don't tell any one you kissed me. It was the champagne got into my head. Good-bye.'

She drew her cloak hurriedly around her, and made a dart across the room, but Galworthy clutched her arm, and held her straining from him, at arm's-length.

'What do you mean?' he asked hoarsely.

'Let me go,' she whispered. 'There is some one coming. For Heaven's sake ——'

A tap fell on the door from without, and silence spread through the room, as it were audibly. Galworthy's heart thumped in his side; Miss Verinder drew herself up quietly, and, covering her head, leaned gently on the window-sill.

'No one shall come in,' he said at length.

The door clamoured under the heavy hands of the impatient visitor.

'Let him knock,' growled Galworthy.

'Why not let him in?' said Betty softly.

Galworthy stared confusedly at her and made no answer. The door shook again.

'Galworthy!' called a voice.

'It's Hampton,' muttered Galworthy.

Miss Verinder moved swiftly from the window, and, gliding noiselessly by him, stood for one moment with her hand on the door-knob. Her eyes met Galworthy's.

'For God's sake!' he cried, under his breath.

She shot back the bolt, and the door flew open, admitting a tall man with a fair beard, who wore his hat on the back of his head and smoked the stump of a cigar.

'Hulloa, Galworthy!' he said; 'why the devil didn't——'

He paused as his glance lighted on Betty.

'Miss Verinder! I beg your pardon!' he exclaimed, snatching vaguely at his hat and his cigar. 'I didn't know any one was here. I——'

Betty broke into her silver laugh.

Galworthy, recovering from his confusion, stepped forward.

'Miss Verinder stopped to leave a note at my door, and—and——'

Betty threw herself back in a chair, and laughed louder than ever.

'My dear Sir Edward,' she said, 'you who know me want no explanations. I'm here, Voilà! What more do you want?'

Hampton stared at her curiously, and in his expression admiration and surprise were blent with a certain shadow of annoyance.

'It's delightful to see you—so unexpectedly,' he said slowly. 'Galworthy is fortunate to——'

Galworthy stood confounded and irresolute. The girl alone seemed undisturbed. She rose and tied the strings of her cloak; with a pretty motion of her shoulders she withdrew her white arms beneath it.

'Were you going?' asked Hampton politely. 'I will find a cab for you.'

Galworthy came forward.

'No,' he said ; 'stay here ; I will go.'

Betty shook her head. 'I think Sir Edward will do it quickest. He has often found cabs for me. You shall tell me your news as we go,' she went on, turning to Hampton. 'How is Lady Hampton? Is she still well?'

He started and a puzzled frown contracted his forehead.

'She was in excellent health when last I heard,' he replied coldly.

'Thanks. I am wonderfully interested in Lady Hampton's health.' Hampton shrugged his shoulders and looked at Galworthy. The latter was still and dumb. 'Come, Sir Edward, I am waiting,' she added.

He tried to meet her eyes, but she had turned towards the door.

'I think, perhaps, Galworthy——' he began.

She stamped her foot. 'If you will not, of course, I can go by myself,' she said shortly.

'Delighted, if Galworthy will excuse me. I'll be back directly.'

'Oh, you're coming back, are you?' she asked.

'Yes,' he answered deliberately. 'There's something I want to talk to Galworthy about.'

'Indeed!' She paused, and fumbled at her throat. She laughed. 'By all means come back,' she said, and her voice had a curious quaver in it. 'Mr. Galworthy requires consoling. It is not every engagement that is made and broken in half an hour.'

Galworthy leaped forward at the words, and glared fiercely and foolishly at Hampton. The latter stopped suddenly on his way to the door, murmured something indistinctly, and then swung slowly out behind her. The sound of their departure faded down the stairs; the front door shut with a bang. Galworthy threw open the window and listened stupidly to the steps receding down the footpath.

It was not until they had reached the corner of the street that Hampton spoke. He stopped and turned upon her quickly.

'Will you tell me what all this means?' he asked coldly. 'Did he ask you to marry him?'

'He did me that honour.'

'And you refused?'

'On the contrary,' she said with a laugh, 'I accepted gratefully. We never imagined our fine little scheme would have been so anticipated, did we? Your presence was quite unnecessary, Edward.'

'Then it is all right?' he inquired eagerly.

'Quite. I have jilted him.'

The man made an exclamation of anger.

'You are intolerable,' he said.

'I really cannot converse all night at street corners,' she replied nonchalantly. 'I have not come to that—yet.'

'Betty!' he said imploringly. 'Betty! Why have you done this?'

She gave him no answer.

'Why?' he insisted.

'Indeed, I 've no mind to marry; that 's all.' He groaned. She burst out laughing. 'What a pretty little plot was ours! and how well you acted! But I did not give you the proper cues. I saw you were put out, but it was a clever performance, a very clever performance. He will never guess.'

'I will see him to-night.'

'I think you will not,' she said smiling.

He looked at her anxiously.

'What are you going to do, Betty?'

'Walk home. The air does me good. It is

a fine night. And is every one quite well?'
She gave a little burst of hysterical laughter.
'How did you say Lady Hampton was when
you heard? I'm mightily interested in Lady
Hampton's health.'

'Betty, Betty! do not talk like that,' he
pleaded earnestly. 'Galworthy was your only
hope, and you've thrown it away. Why—
good Heavens, why?'

She sang a little snatch of song, and put her
hand on his arm.

'Good-bye,' she said.

'What are you going to do,' he asked
anxiously.

'Oh, I don't know.' She laughed again. 'I
think I'll spend the night out of doors, Edward.
Better go home.'

He seized her hand.

'Betty, you are mad. Come with me, dear,
and let everything go.'

She looked at him, and burst into her flute-
like laughter ; then nodding, broke away and ran
up the steps of the house before which they had
paused. Halfway up the steps she threw back
the hood from her face, and her laughter pealed
up to the stars unrestrained and meaningless.

'Good-bye,' she said. 'There's always that Adelphi river, you know.' And pulling up her skirts with one hand, she ran up the remainder of the steps and vanished laughing into the doorway.

IN THE BASEMENT

Two lights contended with the darkness of the room. From the street above the gas shone in a yellow shaft through the dirty little window that peeped upon the area; and from the fading ashes in the hearth the coals glowed obscurely and suffused a timid light. The room itself was full of black corners into which the eyes might peer in vain. The furniture—if indeed the pieces deserved the name—partook of the general blackness. The three chairs were shambling ruins. Each wanted a leg, and the bottom was out of the only one that had ever been proud in cane. Rackety and discoloured past the hue even of floor and ceiling, which were grim with grime, a table rattled to the rumbling of passing carts. The place was thick with evil smells. Odours, veteran and stale with years, clung about the walls; while newer odours of food and spirits and medicine rose as it were from

106

the floor together. On the darkest side of the
room remote from the tiny window the fabric
of a broken bed emerged faintly. Outside and
overhead the stamp of feet along the flags
echoed and faded; the coal-man called; and
the noise of screaming children rose in the
December air.

A sound came suddenly from the squalid bed
along the wall. The two women paused in
their conversation, and looked towards it.

'Poor soul!' said the elder. 'It's a shame
they shouldn't go off more easylike.'

'I dunno when it's goin' to happen,' returned
her companion despondently. 'The doctor—
he says it'll be to-night. But I dunno.'

Her friend sympathised with her. 'It's a
deal o' trouble when you get 'em like that, Mrs.
Williams, and nuthin' coming in. I always says
it's a mercy to be took sudden—that I do.'

'Like what my Jim was,' acquiesced Mrs.
Williams.

'Which one was Jim?'

'Fourth after Bessie Jane. He was a quiet-
like chap too, on'y for the women. He took on
so. I never hardly seen 'im without a collar
round his neck. He fell off of a dray when 'e'd

'ad a drop too much, and the wheel went over 'im. He warn't a bad lad, Jim. That was when we lived Camberwell,' she added meditatively.

'How long was you living Camberwell?' inquired the other woman, with more interest. 'I 'ad a nephew lived there four years.'

'Me and 'im lived there—let's see now. We was there when I was in bed of my seventh—that's Sarah; and we left when my old man took the fever. That must 'a' bin a good ten years, Mrs. Pentecost.'

A low moan issued from the sickbed again, and the speaker got up and stooped over it.

'Lie still, dearie,' she murmured, and she tucked the blanket round the man and patted the pillow soothingly. Then taking her seat once more, she stared reflectively into the fire.

'It's a good thing,' she began after a pause, 'that them insurances was paid up all right last week.'

Mrs. Pentecost assented. 'And the buryin' society too,' she added. 'You ain't lost that either?'

Mrs. Williams was restless; her gaze shifted to the dirty window, and she strained her ears to catch the noises in the street.

'You don't 'ear nothink?' she asked.

'Was you expecting the doctor?'

'No; it's Rebecca Susan—she's coming 'ome to see him 'fore he dies.'

'She done well, has Rebecca Susan,' said Mrs. Pentecost with emphasis, smoothing her lap and edging nearer the fire.

'She's bin parlour-maid three years now in one fambly,' said her mother with some pride.

Mrs. Pentecost rose.   'I'll 'ave to be getting back, Mrs. Williams,' said she.

'You ain't goin' yet,' protested her friend. 'There's plenty o' time. Set down and 'ave a drop o' something.'

'I didn't ought to take it,' said Mrs. Pentecost feebly.   'But I've heard that it's good for as'ma.'

'Law, it'll do you a world of good,' said Mrs. Williams cheerfully.   She rose and bustled about in the darkness.   Somewhere in the recesses of the room a glass clinked.   Mrs. Pentecost's mouth opened, and she moistened her lips.   A fat squat figure wrapt in antic shadows, her hostess crept wheezing out of the gloom, laden with a square bottle, a glass, and a cup without a handle.

'It's comforting to take a drop,' Mrs. Pentecost explained to herself and her friend. Mrs.
Williams poured the spirit into the glass and
the cup. The sick man murmured in his sleep.

'He cries like as he 'ad wind,' said Mrs.
Pentecost compassionately, sipping her gin.

'I s'pose she'll be here direckly,' said Mrs.
Williams, breaking the silence which ensued.

'There's some one stamping on the airey flags
now. That'll be her,' said the other woman.

Both listened ; and then Mrs. Williams got
up, and opening the door of the room, trudged
heavily up the stone stairs. There were sounds
of voices above, the one of a man laughing ;
and clumsy boots descended again into the
basement.

'It's on'y Tom,' said his mother, as she
entered the room.

'On'y me!' said Tom with a silly laugh, as
he followed at her heels. He was a tall young
man, in the dress of a porter ; his face was
flushed, and he stooped a little, so as to keep
his head from brushing against the low ceiling.

'This is bleedin' dark,' he said presently.
''Ow's the old man? He ain't kicked over
yet, 'as 'e?'

'No,' said his mother. 'But 'e ain't going to be here long.'

'Goin' to 'ear the angels,' laughed Tom stupidly, and bent over the bed. ''E ain't goin' to last out much,' he said at length. ''Ullo, father! 'ow d' ye feel? You 'aven't 'ad him shaved?'

The sick man stirred and raised himself weakly on his elbow.

'Jist you lay down, father,' said the woman. 'You ain't fit to set up.'

''Old on, mother; let 'im set up, if he wants to,' said Tom cheerfully. 'He won't be able to get much of what 'e wants, soon enough. You let 'im set up and have a nip of somethink.'

He put his arm round the sick man, and propped him against the wall into a sitting position, while the woman drew the blankets carefully about the withered body.

''Ow d' ye feel yourself, father?' shouted Tom.

'They don't feel much—not so near as this,' commented Mrs. Pentecost thoughtfully.

The invalid opened his mouth as if to answer, but only emitted a hoarse and inarticulate sound.

'Why, 'e ain't got a damn left in 'im,' said

Tom, and turning suddenly to the woman, 'Gawd! you oughter seen me and old Joe this afternoon. We 'ad a pretty sort of row on, *we* did. Strike me, I was in a bloomin' rage. There was a chap come up as we was standin' outside The Sailors—damn his eyes!—and says, whining-like, "Lend me 'arf-a-brown, governor, I 'm starvin'." So I looks at 'im, and he seemed pretty blowed up, so I outs with a copper and claps it into 'is 'and. Then I goes off with Joe into the Three Sailors, you know, just to wet up. And presently who should come in but the bloke 'isself. He didn't see me, so he orders a noggin of gin, and whips out a 'arf-crown, plain as you like. Well, I couldn't stand that. I says to Joe, "I 'm going for 'im," I says. "You bleedin' little tyke," I says, "what d' ye come snivellin' around for a 'a'penny when you got a 'arf-crown in your linings?" I give him beans, I tell you! And I offered to stuff my fingers in his bloomin' face. But he wasn't takin' any —said 'e could get as much as 'e wanted o' that at 'ome. If 'e 'adn't a slipped out, I 'd 'a' laid 'im out—and Joe can tell you.'

'Them fellers has no conscience,' said Mrs. Pentecost sympathetically.

'The dirty dog!' ejaculated Tom. 'Got any gin, mother?'

'No, there ain't no more. Mrs. Pentecost and me 'ad the last.'

'Well, tip us the colour of it, and I'll fetch in some, old woman.'

'Tom, you bring in that shaver, too,' called out Mrs. Williams as he went out of the door. 'If 'e goes off first, we'll 'ave to pay more 'n we like. Them barbers always charges a shilling for a dead,' she explained to Mrs. Pentecost as she took her seat again.

Her friend sighed in sympathy, and there was a temporary silence in the darkening room. Then a thin hoarse voice broke across the stillness.

'D'ye mind that there drive to Peckham Rye, Sally?'

'Gawd love your old bones, course I do,' said Mrs. Williams with emphasis, turning towards the bed.

'Lord, 'ow 'e did startle me!' said Mrs. Pentecost.

'You was that blind drunk afore we got 'ome! And me fallin' out of the shay through laughin',' said the wife.

H

Something that might have stood for a cackle of laughter came from the sick man.

'That was nigh about thirty-three year ago,' Mrs. Williams confided to her friend.

''Ow they do remember!' said Mrs. Pentecost.

'I can't move my 'ead,' said the same hoarse voice.

'You stay up there, father, till the shaver comes. And then we'll let you lay down. Don't you try and move your 'ead.' The man muttered unintelligibly to himself for a little, and then silence fell once more, till it was broken by Mrs. Williams.

'Yes,' she said reflectively. 'It's Gawd's truth. I've seen many of 'em dead, and some die easy and some don't.'

'It ain't as bad as 'avin' a baby, I believe,' said Mrs. Pentecost.

'I dunno, I ain't no opinion about it,' said the wife dully.

'Well, you 'ave your 'usband, and your fambly; and there's a drop of liquor, and a bit o' bread, and a scrag o' mutton, I s'pose—that's what it all comes to,' returned her friend despondently.

'It ain't much more.'

'Not as I want to go just yet—not yet a bit.

And it won't be so 'ard for you 'avin' that buryin' money.'

'I'll give 'im a bit o' gold on 'is coffin,' said Mrs. Williams with some satisfaction.

The noise of feet was heard upon the stairs, and she got up.

''Ere's Tom back with the shaver.' The barber who entered behind her son in an unobtrusive way was a pale young man with hair carefully curled and oiled, and a jaunty appearance of dissipation.

'You ain't got much light,' he remarked, glancing about the room.

'Mother 'll light a candle,' said Tom. The woman bustled into the darkness of a corner, and Tom looked at the barber. The young man still glanced about, and his eye lighted on the glass which stood at Mrs. Pentecost's elbow.

''Ave some along of us?' said Tom cheerily.

'I don't mind,' said the young man. He drank at a draught the gin which Tom poured out. The old woman struck a match, and a feeble light streamed over the bed from a sickly candle.

''E looks pretty groggy,' said the barber doubtfully. 'I dunno but I ought to wait.'

'Oh, 'e's all right.   You walk in,' said Tom.

The young man produced his strop and his razor and approached the sick man.

'Sally, I can't move my 'ead,' whispered the thin voice.

'You shall lay down, father, in a minute,' said his wife encouragingly.

The barber shaved.

Tom took his seat near the fire, and emptied some gin into a tumbler.

''Ave some more, Mrs. Pentecost?' he said.

The woman declined.

'Mother, you come along and 'ave some,' he called.

The wife moved from the bedside and came to the fire.

'I won't 'ave none,' she replied abstractedly. She sighed. ''Ow people do change! He ain't a bit like what 'e was when we was married.'

'That's a tidy long time ago, mother.'

'Thirty-five year and four months.'

'You got it straight enough.'

'Well, it ain't what one would be likely to forget, any more'n the first baby,' said Mrs. Pentecost.

' 'Ow old was Jim when 'e fell off of the dray?' asked Tom, sipping his gin.

' Nigh on twenty-five, he was.'

The sound of the razor ceased, and Tom looked round.

' Finished?' he asked.

' Yes,' said the young man doubtfully, and stood looking down upon his subject.

Tom and his mother approached the bed.

' You lay 'im down again sideways,' said the mother. ' It 'll be easier for 'im. Why, 'e 's fell over a bit,' she said in surprise.

Tom looked at the barber. His mother bent down and took hold of her husband's hand.

' What are you layin' down like that for, old man?' she asked. ' What you got your 'ead so tight agin' that nasty board for? Just you set up, and we 'll lay you down. You 'll ketch cold.'

' You shut up, mother!' said Tom roughly. ''E 'll never want no more layin' down, but one. 'E 'll never ketch no more cold—'e won't.'

The woman started and raised herself, staring upon the body in silence.

' I knowed 'e was dead,' said the barber. ' I knowed 'e was dying when I come in. That makes it a bob.'

'You better get out!' said Tom angrily. 'It ain't going to be a bob, and so I tell you flat. You better look slippy!'

The dissipated young man mumbled, glanced at the tall figure, and finally disappeared through the door.

Tom sat down opposite Mrs. Pentecost.

'Damned cheek!' he muttered.

'Ain't you better cover up his face?' whispered Mrs. Pentecost hoarsely.

Tom shook his head. 'I dunno.   Mother'll do that.'

The woman stood by the bed; she reached down and chafed the stiffening fingers of the dead man's hand.   Then she left the bedside, and moved towards her two companions.

''E ain't much like what he used to be when I knew 'im first,' she said in a vague voice.

'Sit down, now do,' pleaded Mrs. Pentecost. 'Rest yourself, and 'ave a drop more.   It'll stiddy your nerves.'

Mrs. Williams paid no attention to this request.   She looked vacantly into the fire.

'Rebecca Susan ain't come after all,' she said.

Tom poured himself out another glass of gin.

AN ORDEAL OF THREE

I COULD not be mistaken. The breath of the soft air was in my hair and on my forehead, but a softer breath still lingered on my face. The warm sun glowed upon my cheeks, but my lips were burning with a fresher warmth. The long culms of the grasses rustled in my ears, but something more delicate and gracious still stirred about me. I could have no possible doubt of some presence by my side. Slowly the drowsy wits came back to life, with this subtly sweet impression, and with a start were suddenly alert and anxious. I sat up and listened; the swish of skirts sounded distantly; and in a second I had realised the event. The place was still fragrant as from some new-blown flower. I leapt to my feet and darted into the little wood.

When I came out breathless upon the high-walled garden, I stopped in perplexity at the division of the pathways. I had not been prepared for so bewildering an answer to my puzzle; for there before me were all three, equally dispassionate, as it seemed, and equally unalarmed. Her stately form invested with fresh green leaves, Dorothy caressed the holly-hocks, as tall and royal as herself. On the mid-path stood Cynthia smelling at the roses, her white gown blowing in the breeze; while dainty Joan was bent low over the carnations, a very mirror of pensive meditation. It was into this atmosphere of still repose I burst in rude excitement. Joan glanced up quickly at my voice; Cynthia turned to meet me; Dorothy remained motionless beside the hollyhocks. The problem at once grew grave and im-portunate. Which of the three had it been?

Cynthia greeted me with a smile and a charming little toss of her head.

'So you are awake at last,' said she. 'I saw you sprawling from a distance. 'Twas not of your proper courtesy to leave us so ungenerously upon a fine afternoon.'

She made a tiny grimace, in which it seemed I must read something more significant. My heart thumped. Could it be then that she of her grace had condescended so? She broke into laughter that wrinkled her eyes. I felt I could be content it should be Cynthia.

'Heavens, what a serious face!' she cried. 'If you have no conversation to save us from moping it shall not be I will keep you company. You were best rubbing your eyes.'

She turned on her heel and left me, and I sighed with a sudden doubt. She was scarce likely to make so bold with her tongue had she indeed been guilty. Soberly I took my way to Dorothy across the borders.

'Ah!' said she, with a glance from her flowers. 'You have come in the hour of my need. Would maids were of a size convenient! Pray reach me the topmost flower.'

I did her bidding, and she smiled upon me graciously.

'And where have you been?' said she, wrapping her nosegay round.

'This,' thought I, as I gave her some opportune answer, 'is surely but the ignorance of knowledge. Her attitude of ease, and her aspect of indifference are too severe and careful to be natural. She speaks calmly out of her many tremors, and could I inspect her heart I should find it quaking and ashamed.'

'You are dull to-day,' she said presently; 'a useful servant, but a cheerless companion. Do you admire my nosegay? Oh! this garden is afire; I'll seek the orchard,' and with that she faded away.

I watched her go, but she betrayed no haste, and her gait was as queenly and secure as ever. Could it, indeed, be that one who wore this dignity of embarrassed kindliness had so far stooped from her frigid height? I dared not think it and went off, all ashamed of my insolent thought, to pretty Joan, the last of the three. The last—but the likeliest? I thought she flushed slightly as I stayed beside her without salutation. The silence seemed even to disturb her. She shifted uneasily under my gaze.

'Oh, 'tis hot, 'tis hot,' said she, smoothing back the tumbled hairs from her brow. 'And I to feel it so who have this moment come from the house!'

I assented that it was hot, and mopped my own forehead, as I meditated upon the import of this speech. She has confessed, I reflected exultantly; she has confessed by her very anxiety to disprove her neighbourhood. Plainly

it was she; and as I regarded her closely,
I could be glad that it was no other. She
threw a sly glance at me.

'You have lost your tongue,' said she. 'You
are as much confounded as though you had just
risen;' and she shook her head smilingly at me.

But this again set me back wandering among
doubts, as one might not be so bold and yet so
timid in a breath. No, I reflected, gazing after
her, it was surely not this demure creature,
whose soul is ever in her eyes, whose innocence
is as conspicuous as the dimple in her cheek.
She had not so far dared even for the love of me.
And here I was brought to pause by a primary
consideration in my problem. Was the act of
love, of malice, or of accident? If of love, perchance after all it was Joan; but if of malice,
then Cynthia for a crown; while if it were
Dorothy, I could conceive it nothing but the
unexpected outcome of some odd mischance.
And yet if love, why not any of the three, since
love will venture anything, and betray into the
most wonderful surprises? 'Let us say it was
love,' I said, 'certainly some guilty mark will
suddenly reveal her to me.' And to that end
throughout the summer day I kept a watch

upon them. Did one look at me I was still contemplating the sky, indifferent-wise, to outward seeming, every sense strained to interpret that glance. Did one laugh, out of the corner of my eye I observed every line and wrinkle of her smile. I beset them with careless attentions ; they might not move without my regard : each little exhibition of human emotion I tracked to its original and lawful home. But, alas! I made nothing by my persistence, for every act of all refuted its predecessor. There was no order in my conclusions ; the one perverted another ; and half a dozen times an hour I must form and reform my verdict. A thousand kisses had not cost me so much embarrassment. Dorothy's eyes were placidly content, and never rested upon me of premeditation ; I suspected her. Cynthia laughed full and meaningly into my face : of her too I had grave suspicion. Joan shot bashful glances from below her drooping lashes : I could have sworn it was she.

'She who loves me,' said I, 'will take my gift in some intimate manner.' I made each the offer of a flower—a rose to Cynthia, a passionless lily to Dorothy, a red carnation to blushing Joan. Dorothy gave me a gentle smile and fingered her lily prettily; Cynthia pressed her rose to her lips; Joan hid her blossom in her heaving bosom. Was there then nothing by which she might be known? By this I was grown desperate, and determined upon bolder measures. I dared not put the question to them patently, but I might lead each slowly to some situation of my contrivance, and perchance confronting her with the ghost of her own impertinence might convict the offender of her dear offence.

We sat in the falling light around the table. Dorothy looked out of the window upon the lawn, and Joan admired the eglantine. Cynthia yawned and played with her knife. I took a glass of wine.

'I love not a prude,' said I, breaking the silence. 'I have always had a distaste for untimely modesty. Women,' I said, 'have no quality more delightful than the tact which will instruct them when to dispense with reserve. Should they choose to condescend from their imperial reticence, the liberty does them infinite service; it is a parcel of their sovereignty. I would make no complaint, though one were to strip herself of all the modes and manners of society and come habited in audacities of her own. Nay, the act would be individual in her.'

Dorothy stared at me ; Cynthia stared at me ; they stared at me all three.

' This is to prove, sir?' says Cynthia roguishly.

' Proprieties are odious on occasion,' I observed. ' I would have you understand that this is my creed. I am all for a free spirit.'

' Indeed,' says Dorothy with a smile. ' It is good of you to inform us of this.'

' Heigho !—a sermon,' quoth Cynthia with a pretty yawn ; 'and to-morrow Sunday !'

Joan dimpled. ' Is there no more?' she asked with gentle archness.

' For a man to kiss a maid,' I resumed without wincing, 'is natural and just. Why, then, serve not a maid with the same sauce ? If the chance befall her and fit her humour, in God's name let her kiss and be merry.'

Dorothy shifted her chair and drummed her foot upon the floor ; Joan blushed and glanced away ; Cynthia burst into a peal of laughter.

' You are too kind !' she cried. ' But 'tis well we have your permission. We owe you thanks. Perhaps also we have now the liberty to withdraw.'

The door clapped to behind them. I sat staring moodily into my wine.

'If this will not serve,' I said angrily, 'then shall they have it in all seriousness, and the Devil take the responsibility. I will make love, and be damned to it ; and I 'll wager the pretty maid that loves me will come tumbling into my arms this very evening. So surely shall I discover and unmask her.'

When I leaned across the window-sill and murmured into Dorothy's ear, the dusk was falling, and the odour of fir-trees was in the air. I spoke of courtly queens and royal maidens, of golden hair and quiet, serious eyes. 'Those things,' I said, 'are dear to me, constituents of my high ideal. I have the desire to be done with the dolorous delights of wayward days. There comes a time in the affairs of youth when the man must discard unworthy follies, and steal home to the heart that loves him.'

Much more I said, being now astride my counterfeit passion. She heard me silently, and sighed.

'Ah, to live and love!' she murmured. 'It completes the serenity of life,' and sighed again.

I took her hand. She looked into my face; smiling beatitudes sighed from her lips. She rose and glided gently from the room.

And now it seemed that I was at last at the solution of my problem; but yet I must go the round rather from a sense of logic than out of any lingering doubt. And so it came to pass that in the mellow twilight I sat watching Cynthia's scarlet lips part and close and part again. I had thought to have no taste for the encounter, but the sight somehow set me aglow to be nearer her. I fell in with the chase of her mad whims, and together we raced about a tiny world which for the nonce was all our own. Then at a pause I broke into the hot words of my declaration. 'For me,' quoth I, 'no staid and sluggish spirit. I love a full-souled ardent gaze, of a warm and ruddy passion, lithe jocund limbs, and the fretting fever of desire. An I were sure of such, how much happiness were mine!'

She returned me my look of longing, her eyes sparkled, the light danced over her face.

'Yes,' said she suddenly, 'and such love were worth all—to a woman.'

Her hand dangling by her chair, I seized and

bore half-way to my lips. I thought the pressure was returned ; she rose and fled the terrace.

Left to myself, I passed up and down in per-plexity. Was mortal man ever so horribly dis-traught ? By all the signs it should be this one that had loved me and embraced me in the meadows. Now I thought upon it, Dorothy's smile struck me as something impartial, her sigh as merely dutiful, her words as wholly tolerant. The fervour of Cynthia's mood seized openly upon me. In Joan I looked for nothing save maybe a little exhibition of panic at the bold advertisement of love. But she must still be tested according to my vow, and forthwith I set out to find her.

It was in the tail of the gloaming that I stooped over her chair and drew slowly into in-timacy by sundry words of sympathy. She was all bashfulness and virgin modesty, moved from me gently, turned her glance aside, fidgeted with her flower, and finally, when I had ex-hibited in full my affection for a shy and cling-ing nature, and had grown emboldened to touch her fingers, withdrew softly from my vicinity.

'I wish you good fortune,' she whispered. 'Such an one would be very happy with her.'

I

Dumfounded I sat upon the terrace and blinked stupidly at the stars in a maze of conflicting opinions. If ever the tokens of a tender affection were anywhere visible, they were worn upon the embarrassment of this maid. The last venture had left me no less confident than the others; and Cynthia's lips had faded with Dorothy's eyes. The more I reflected the more serious and difficult did the paths of my deduction grow, the further was I from any disentanglement. I had tried all the avenues of knowledge and was now no wiser. I raised my hands to heaven in my disgust to be no better judge of feminine conduct. Had I been discerning there was certainly some mute witness to convict the dainty sinner. But I had gone hunting all the day with all my wits and senses and still was at a loss to find it.

'The Devil take it!' said I in my chagrin, 'I will yet be at the end of this puzzle. Not a sign of embarrassment that may discover her, but she shall wear it by my contrivance. I have been long-suffering, I have taken the task with too great a patience, and too signal a modesty. I will now dare all and meet her with her own audacity.'

In this resolve I spent the morning, but it was late ere I had mustered spirit for the new enterprise. A thousand considerations blocked the way. I must secure each apart, and in a proper disposition. To each I must approach in a different fashion; with each must renew my confidences of the twilight. And again, I was beset by prickings of my conscience, lest what I was to undertake should be an act discourteous, should lay too onerous an obligation on the lady. But these doubts and difficulties vanished at last. 'It is only meet,' I mused, 'to inflict on her her own penalty; and if in the process of justice two innocents be involved also in the sentence, why, they suffer for their company, and have no cause of complaint, and this is how I shall know her. She will surely return,' said I, 'my kiss, and as she kissed me in the meadow, so will her lips touch mine, responsive to my caress.' . . .

I sought my room distracted. Alas! Conceive me plunged deeper and deeper in the toils of wonder, further and further in the recesses of despair. I know not which lips were the softer; I know not which were the warmer; I know not which of the three returned me my kiss the most readily or the most tenderly.

THE PORTRAIT IN THE INN

HIS extreme resemblance to myself struck me anew as I looked at him. The identity in our personal appearance had been wont to bother me from time to time, as one who continually saw his double mimicking before him. As boys, I remember, we were both indifferent to our likeness, and I fancy that he carried his disregard into his adult life. If he reflected upon it at all, it was certainly with amusement, for he had a trick of inconsequent laughter and took the accidents of the world with a very smiling gaiety, which I had always envied. But for myself—the knowledge of this twin, when I had him to my face, was a vague discomfort. It seemed preposterous that Nature should have stooped to the jest, when her devices were so prodigal elsewhere. We had the self-same smile; the self-same expressions marked the self-same features. We were cast in one mould with a nicety foreign to her general practice.; and if we diverged it was in some private particulars undiscovered even of our friends. The set and habit of our frames and countenances were in perfect unison, and yet I think in every direction our characters had taken opposite courses. This disparity within so close a resemblance had given me a grudge against the coincidence, as I could not but think of it as a grotesque freak whereby we were more for the amusement than the wonder of our friends. Something of this annoyance possessed me as I noted the merry manner and complacent temper with which he dwelt upon his news.

'I wish you luck,' said I, 'the best of luck, Philip. I suppose the thing was inevitable. At thirty-two this sort of fact is very near. If you had got beyond that age safely, you might have gone to your grave a decent bachelor.'

'*You* are still there,' said he with a grin. The reminder irritated me, but I had never the heart to visit my peevishness upon him. I smiled.

'True,' I answered, 'I'm not a braggart yet; it is only the voice of philosophy speaks in me. As for myself, I have imagined the grand passion, as you will phrase it, and have its dimensions pretty well by heart. But that, I take it, is the safest insurance against it.'

'I don't see it,' he replied, as though he would dispute my point, but, having little of a head for argument, struck out impulsively upon a theme that was more to his liking. 'I can't see your prejudice against love. It's divine; it's immortal. Heaven! how it thrills a man, Dick! You have only got to furnish yourself with my soul for a day, and you 'll spend the rest of your life eating your words.'

'Love,' said I, 'is admirable after dinner.'

'It's an infamy,' he broke out, 'it's a sacri-lege, a blasphemy. That I should have a brother born to such feelings! And outwardly we are replicas,' he ended with a laugh.

'I believe in your love,' said I, 'but I can't fit it into my life. I think I should ask a miracle with mine. I have, my dear fellow, every desire and ambition to be married, but the thing hangs fire; there is no Prometheus.'

'Well, well; you will have it one day,' he concluded, and fell to his raptures again. I let him run on, scarcely heeding his enthusiasms, for my thoughts had turned inwards upon myself and my own flat life. I had but newly recovered from a long illness, and had come back to the world with no particular zest for living. The convalescence to which in my extremest hours of pain I had looked forward with delight had been fulfilled drearily enough; and now that once more I had the liberty of the streets the occupations and interest of the prospect seemed stale and empty. It was perhaps a condition of the body; I know, at least, it was no healthy, natural distaste that possessed me. But the effort of existence appeared too severe for the reward, and I could not imagine myself informed with any individual interest. I drew out of these miserable reflections to find him silent, and scanning me with some affectionate concern.

'Are you quite yourself now?' he asked.

'In excellent health,' I answered; 'only a little astonished at the zeal with which I fought for life. Is there anything worth the struggle, my dear Philip? Is there anything—save this love of yours?' I added with a smile.

He invited me cheerfully to be his companion on his journey. He was going, it appeared, to

Paris for a few weeks; thence returning to his lady-love with all the hot-foot ardour of his kind. I excused myself with my best grace; his vigour promised to appal me, and I was best unembarrassed, I thought. Ere he left he had resumed his extravagant mood of happiness, was pressing me with invitations to call upon the lady's family, and was begging me to follow his wise example. And when he finally got away it was to run down the steps with a peal of laughter, and all the light-heartedness of a schoolboy.

The matter of his visit was not of inordinate moment, and yet thoughts induced by it strayed persistently through my brain. What, I reflected, if it were possible, after all, to acquire a fresh interest in the world by this simple procedure of marriage? I had made an experiment over many years in the single state, and at the end could not boast my fortune. I could scarcely see how, at the close of an equal term, it were easy to be in a worse case. Indeed, the change, since it was to something, might import some new faiths and feelings with its facts; might indue me with a novel vitality; might arrest that decline upon a mechanical round in which there were few distractions and fewer pleasures, and which now seemed to be my prospect. The fancy struck suddenly to my heart, as a flash; for one second of time I felt the warmth of the convert thrilling through my body, and then the sensation trailed off in incredulity. There had been a point of fascination in it, but it came only to a chance of the instant, as it were, through a chink from an invisible, imaginary world full of light and mystery. Forthright it faded from my mind without restraint, and there was the world again before me, as dull and as indifferent as ever.

But the dog-days were hard upon us, and I must needs be packing for some fresher air than London's. It would have saved me a score of small worries had I fallen in with Philip's invitation, and several times in the next fortnight I recalled it with regret. I had no desire to be off, but the change grew inevitable as the days wore on, and after all the disposition of my body mattered little; I should be still in the possession of the same disconsolate spirit. I scarcely knew what had directed my choice of the seaside. For one thing I was averse from a trip abroad, merely, I think, because the distance would put me to a longer discomfort. And the sea, at this time, should be full of breezes pleasant enough to face. But it was with little elation I got aboard my train, and turned my attention idly to the morning papers, in which I had already failed to discover a single thread of interest. The sun shone hotly upon the meadows, and within the narrow confines of my carriage I grew clammy and restless. Three hours of such a passage seemed likely to drive me frantic. I had no fellow-passengers; not a page in my volumes drew my interest; the landscape with its flying monotony of hedges, elms, and fields became as obvious and as unassertive to the sight as the rattle of the train to my ear. The telegraph poles, shooting past at settled intervals, as it were with perceptible sound, at first an amiable interruption, came soon to be a part of the mechanical monotony by which I was surrounded. At the close of an hour I had lost the passive resignation with which I had set out, and was fretting against the limits of my position. We had reached Northorpe, I think, when I half formed the resolution to abandon my journey. I was out on the platform with my baggage, my mind rocking somewhat irresolutely betwixt the two ideas, when the train suddenly took the decision upon itself and slipped out of the station.

It was a mean and petty village at which I had alighted ; how it had achieved the dignity of a station I cannot say. There was no house had a look of consequence in the place. The country ran into many ridges in the neighbour-hood, and deep woods lay in patches on the summits of those heights. But saving for this outlook upon a broken landscape the village itself lacked beauty. I found a fair inn of a rustic sort, at which I stored my property ; and then set out for a walk upon the hills.

It was late in the evening ere I returned, pretty tired, from my ramble. The landlord, who had, it appeared, fallen from a better posi-tion, served me himself, and grew talkative over his task. The house was but little frequented, I was informed ; was larger than it should be ; but had fulfilled other purposes in the coaching days. He had only the village from which to draw his custom, and some such stray visitor as myself. He commended to me a bottle of his best wine, which I found he had hardly over-praised, and left me, finally, to it and my own thoughts. The dusk had fallen ere I finished my meal, and throwing open the window which overlooked a pretty strip of garden, I turned up the lamp and lay back in my chair with my cigar. The light shone diffusely upon the walls of the long room, which I perceived were adorned with numerous prints, most of old date, mainly pictures of horses and masters of hounds, but some of more recent and German origin— rude oleographs and terrible engravings. But one there was, of a different character from its neighbours, that arrested my wandering attention. The thing was not ill-done, though it was by no means good; but it was the face that held my eyes. The girl was dressed in summer white, her collar loosened about her throat as though the day were sultry; and she looked forth at me, leaning upon the gate of a meadow. The expression of her features was wistful and silent; it was as though she desired to speak and was yet dumb; her eyes searched me; her lips were parted in a rift of eagerness. The face was of a beauty so delicate that it caught and stayed my breath; out of the flat paper it regarded me with its immeasurable eyes. The gaze haunted me.

The wine I had drunk had lifted me from my dreamy state of indifference, and the prospect of the morrow did not rise so blackly in my mind. There was a kind of pleasure even in the green trees, the quiet pool, the slow rustling of the elms before the inn. I rose from my chair and moved to the window. Outside, the night, which had fallen thick with stars, was very peaceful. A cool wind played about the garden plot ; a cow was lowing over the meadows from some byre. For the first time for a twelvemonth I had the feeling of content. I turned and looked about the room, and the eyes of that picture were watching me softly, appealingly. The flame sank in the lamp, and, diverted by the accident, I crossed to the table and turned up the wick. As I did so I raised my head, and the eyes looked towards me beseechingly. A little thrill passed down me; I went straight to the wall and stared into the picture. I could have fancied that the parted lips were opened a little further, that the eyes beamed a little brighter, that the air of that face grew more sprightly. The fancy was strong upon me. I sat down at the table.

'Here,' said I, turning to her with my lifted glass—'Here, sweet, I will drink to your eyes. I have come to this place, a stranger in need of sympathy, and they have given me welcome. Your face has smiled down upon me at my solitary meal; your lips have striven to converse with me; your eyes have watched me incessantly throughout this evening. Dear, you have kept me company with the prettiest of faces. I should be a boor to deny you this toast. To you, sweetheart, even to you, who have come betwixt me and the devil this night, I drain this glass. To your eyes, my beloved, to your eyes.'

The picture smiled at me; but still the bosom leaned upon the gate, the hands still clasped each other over the topmost rail; still the eyes searched me wistfully and dreamily, as though they were looking for some one that came not. I rose in my seat.

'Dear,' said I, 'I will come. Is it for me you keep so steadfast a watch? Is it for me your pensive eyes look out into the dusk? You shall wait no longer. You have, my dearest, turned a doubter into the most ardent of lovers.'

I burst into laughter. The wine seemed to have gone to my head, and yet I had drunk but little. The blood rushed along the arteries and my pulse ticked in my forehead like a clock. The face watched me slowly from the room.

I had the whim to bid her good-bye in the morning, which I did with equal ceremony. I had thought that the peculiar impression I had taken from so common a print would have worn off by daylight, that the face would convince me merely of an indiscretion in my wine, not of its own distinctive qualities. And I got a little queer shock to find the pleasure renewed —a shock not disagreeable, but very sudden and odd. When I left Northorpe later in the day, I had settled upon no destination. As it chanced I took the train a little further towards my seaport, got half an hour or so upon my way, and finally descended upon a hamlet in the thick of some forest-land. Its name I have forgotten, but that is of little consequence. I had the choice of inns on this occasion, and decided for one that stood at the foot of a black strip of pine-wood, on a certain elevation, somewhat remote from the noises of the village.

It put me in a better temper to be spending my holiday after so eccentric a fashion ; and, moreover, the air was fine, the roads were excellent, and here, too, I had an admirably wholesome dinner. The lights faded out from the west, the skyline of which was ragged with waving trees ; and after the inns had emptied and the sounds of the departing villagers retired into silence, I took another stroll through the churchyard. The moon was rising very gravely ; the stars shone like jewels ; a stream ran with a soft music at the bottom of the acre. I leaned over the footbridge and stared into the water. In this running brook I could see faces gathering and dissolving ; many stories glinted out of the mirror upon me. My own face lay upon the water in a black patch of shadow, seeming to take part in these drifting histories. But it was in vain that I tried to follow one to its end. No sooner had I the glimpse of its motive than the tale itself was gathered into the eddies and floated down the stream in a tangle of lights and shadows. The clock in the belfry struck eleven ; a rook complained from its neighbouring colony ; I yawned and went back to bed.

The moonlight was striking direct through my window, and lay so brightly on the floor that I did not trouble to use my candle, but undressed by the pale glamour. I had been, I suppose, an hour asleep when I awoke with a feeling of restlessness. The night had grown warmer, and I rolled about in my bed to find a position cool enough for stillness; but my efforts were vain, and at last I lit a candle and read. It must have been some ten minutes later that, glancing up from my book, I found myself staring at the picture. It hung upon the wall at the foot of my bed, and the eyes were bent upon me with the self-same wistfulness that had touched my fancy on the previous evening. I started at the sight and the volume dropped upon the floor; but the eyes rested upon my face. A warm flush of sensation, something between pain and desire, throbbed through my body. It was, of course, but a coincidence; these prints were the common property of the countryside. Yet the instant repetition of a face that had made so deep and so recent a mark upon my mind filled me with a kind of awe. That face was sacrosanct and virgin, and it yearned for me. I gazed intently

K

for awhile, and then a sort of tenderness in-spired my blood. I kissed my hand with a little laugh under my breath.

'Good-night,' said I, 'fair mistress. And so you will even keep ward upon me here too. Dear, you have been much in my thoughts; your face has crept about with me all day, and now you are here in the flesh to comfort me. How long have you waited?' I asked; 'how many weary hours have you watched for your coming lover?'

I blew out the light and fell asleep in a curious content. The night passed lightly, but in my dreams the face came and went. I could scarcely say I had been dreaming, for there was no sense of time or sequence in my visions; only that face recurred at intervals, lighting and fading, as a magic portrait cast upon a screen. I have slept more soundly, but never, I think, with a greater possession of pleasure.

The re-apparition dwelt in my thoughts the best part of the following day. A feeling of pure delight kept occupying my soul. I seemed, in a word, to have taken some strange elixir by which I was lifted quite out of my apathy.

The face made its home with me ; I had it as
surely printed upon my memory as it was upon
the artist's paper. And what was more, with
these two surprises I was in secure expectation
of another. I should meet it again for certain ;
at my next inn it would confront me as pathe-
tically and as sweetly as now. I had the whim
that it mattered nothing where I went, where
I was to rest next—the picture would greet me
there without fail. I laughed cheerfully to myself as I considered my plans for the day, and
finally made my next stage a place exceedingly
distant, a tiny village in the west, picked out
at a guess on the maps, at which I arrived late
in the evening, very dusty and overtired. You
may not conceive my disappointment when I
found my picture was not here. The sense of
vacancy that fell numb upon me was a witness
to the sorry condition of my nerves, showed
how far the mad humour had got into my blood.
There was no sign of her in the house, and
with a grimace at my own folly I strove to
dismiss the absurd fantasy from my mind.

The place was pretty enough, and was in the
height of summer perfection. Rain had fallen
overnight, and the pleasant smell of earth was

abroad in the air. The day I spent in wandering without special intention, listening to the gossips, and half finishing plans for the future. I had walked out upon the common, which ran on a pretty steep incline to the hills, and near about five in the afternoon was feeling somewhat of fatigue. At the border of the common were some smiling meadows, in one of which I took refuge from the sun, throwing myself under the shelter of a grove of ash-trees. I must have fallen asleep, for when I awoke the westering sun was retiring from the valley, and the air was much cooler. The prospect of golden lights was so fine, and I had recovered so much from my snatch of sleep, that I sat up, the better to take in its beauties. As I did so I grew aware of a neighbour, and turning my head saw some one at the gate.

The sudden impression of my discovery upon me was so startling that my eyes were held by the vision while you might have counted a minute. She had taken off one glove, as she was shown in the picture; her hands were clasped together; her face, bent forward, was turned a little from me, with the familiar aspect of that visiting print. There was not one particular I could note to divorce her from the portrait. An exclamation sprang from my lips as I rose to my feet, and at the sound she moved her head and saw me. Just as it had happened in my dreams these past two days, so now she gave a little cry of welcome, a smile ran over her features, she made as though to open the gate that stood between us. As she fumbled with the latch I drew near like one walking in shadowland, watching her face with fearful admiration. But at this the wraith, as I had half imagined her, broke into a merry laugh.

'How you have stared!' said she; then stopped and regarded me anxiously.

The fall of her voice on the soft evening air stirred me from my reverie, and I perceived her on a sudden to be truly corporeal and very proximate. There was no spark of wonder lit my eyes as I took her hand and gazed into her blue orbs steadfastly; no flash of awe held me silent. The event had come, it seemed, as of nature; that she and I should be there together, that she had waited for me at the gate as she had waited in the picture, seemed to me as right and inevitable as life itself, or death.

'Dear,' I said, 'I have come at last.' I took her face between my hands and scanned it closely, drinking from the deeps of its gay beauties. 'How I have dreamed of you! How often have I seen your face like this!'

She laughed, a trifle nervously, as though struck with a sudden diffidence; but nestling to me the next moment met my look with happy rapture.

'You were so long,' she murmured tenderly. I kissed her lips. The valley was full of soft, burning scents; the light stood on the highest hill-tops. Her skirts shook in the breeze, and her breaths rustled the bodice on her bosom. There was a deep and peaceful silence about us. I held her to me tightly, my hand smoothing the warm flesh of her cheeks.

'How long you have been away!' she said; 'and was Paris so very full of attractions?'

The words fell upon dull ears. I scarcely took their meaning. She continued—

'You are strange,' she said, 'and changed, Philip.'

I started, but I still held her face to me. 'You have grown more serious,' she went on. 'Is anything wrong, dear?' and looked up at me with so enchanting a timorousness as to set my heart throbbing heavily.

'Nothing,' I said, 'nothing ; but I love you, I love you.'

Her voice rose and sank through my dreams —sweet and gay; the while I had her folded to me, listening as some one far away to her talk and the confidences of her pure soul. In truth I had fallen suddenly from heaven upon hell. The gift that some providence or benign chance had sent me I had taken without question or wonder, for it had seemed to issue straight from my precedent surprises ; I had risen to the proper emotion as one prepared and forewarned. And now in an instant I had lost my pre-eminence, my joy fled from me at a stroke, and I perceived that I was but a factor in a grotesque and horrid joke played upon me by coincidence. And as I stood there upon the margin of the field, with all high heaven singing above me, and the fairest scene ever set by nature spread before my eyes, the memory of Philip's rapture, the rush of his eager words, the name and praise of his lady-love, returned to me as vividly as though I were listening to his voice. I knew her name

—this ardent miracle of beauty; her descent, her private history, the details of her environment were all now in my knowledge. She was twenty some three months back; she was the only daughter of the squire; she had a devout attachment to her lover; she was the most innocent, the most bewitching of her sex. As these thoughts burned in me like molten lead I laughed in my bitterness and pushed her from me roughly. Her face took on a look of quick perplexity and distress. How her emotions ran upon her features!

'You are changed, Philip,' said she.

I pulled her to me, laughing wildly.

'My dearest, changed only in this, that I love you now with the heat of fever.'

I kissed her in my madness, and she surrendered herself shrinkingly to me. 'This thing,' I cried in my heart, 'has gone beyond me. I will see the end, whatever it be.' Philip and his merry laughter vanished out of my mind. I took her arm and we went forth together, happy and unafraid. She babbled sweetly of the flowers, of some pets, old friends of mine, of her generous father, of different people of that vicinity with whom I was acquainted. And wrapt in my happiness I listened, walking by her side, filling my soul with her loveliness, and thinking nothing of the morrow. I can remember how the squire met me, with his cheerful face. His talk was simple, of dogs and horses, and his garden; but it seemed to me he was speaking deep wisdom. I must try 'Crusader' again, he declared; my feat had been the wonder of the countryside. Poor Dorothy had flown into a fury when he had vowed I should take the jump again; and, that availing nothing, into tears. He laughed. I looked at Dorothy. Her face, surmounted with a hot flush, met my eyes as though entreating me to pardon and humour her frailty.

'I think,' said I, '"Crusader" must look for another rider.'

She thanked me with a clap of her hands and a smile. And I—I laughed sardonically, for Philip, gay and reckless, came debonairly across my vision.

That evening was one of superlative charm. My bags were fetched (from the station, I explained), and we dined in state in the merriest of humours. My return must be celebrated, quoth the squire, clinking his glass gleefully

154 THE PORTRAIT IN THE INN

against Dorothy's; the old wine was produced from the deepest cellar, and we drank to our common happiness and devotion. I cannot recall that I had one single twinge of conscience that night. How was it possible, with Dorothy laughing in her arm-chair, and despatching glances of singular sweetness and intimate confidence across the room to me? I talked as I had never talked for years; all my old wit and knowledge came back to my service. I felt I held the room, nor was I mistaken. The squire stared and winked over his glass. I had more in my head, he confessed, than he had ever fancied; I was eloquent—that's what he would say; and upon his soul I should stand for the county. And Dorothy clapped her hands and listened, with her head against her father's arm, watched me with eyes of deep and growing affection. Now and then she would peep into the squire's face, as though to remark his astonishment at my talk, and her own glance sparkled with admiration. And when the hours had worn on, and she rose to leave us, she took me to the door.

'Philip,' she whispered, 'you have made me very happy, dear—very happy '

Very happy! cried the room from all its corners; very happy! murmured the elms out on the lawn; very happy! said my heart, in answer. I sat down to keep the squire company, the words ringing in my ears. If only this had been from the first! If only it were now to continue! I drank that night deeply, and the old man kept me in countenance. But the joy had intoxicated me more than the wine, and I went to bed singing a snatch of some glad old love-song of the South.

The morning brought me no sobriety. At dawn I was wandering upon the lawn under her window, picking the freshest rose for her bosom. We rode and walked that day, each wrapt in the other's fellowship. The squire troubled us little, being a master of small ceremonies on his estate, and there was no one to put an embargo upon our reckless impulses. At times I strove to turn and face my position, but the efforts ended without a definite achievement. I reasoned, too, with myself, and persuaded my own conscience. She loved me, it was clear, and, indeed, more dearly than ever, as she confessed. The trick had been played us both by a whimsical fate, and were I to discover my proper individuality, she still loved me. An extreme resemblance had started her on the mistake, and now who was to say whether her love was Philip or I? Were both to stand before her, would she not choose at a venture, haphazard; if indeed she did not hit upon me, in whom she had discovered new virtues and larger powers? So I consoled my scruples, with no thought for the tragedy that was at hand.

It was on the second day, midway between noon and the fall of dusk, that the end came. We were upon the lawn, near the little arbour of trees that overlooked the heath. She had plucked some forget-me-nots and was fastening them into my coat when I heard the sound of feet, and, looking up, saw him coming down the garden walk with his sprightliest manner. But she heard and saw nothing, for she was chatting prettily as she inserted the flowers, and at that moment he turned off upon the grass and his approach was noiseless. I think he did not take us in at the outset, but presently, pulling up with a start when some twenty paces away, stared open-mouthed upon me. She chattered sweetly in my ears; my eyes watched him unflinchingly; I made no sign of recognition. I can feel now the haze that crept over my wits, the hollow that formed quickly in my heart. But he threw up his hands, nodded once or twice swiftly, as though he had at last found some clue to the mystery of our relations; signalled to me privately, and then, stalking stealthily along the lawn, made towards us without a sound. My gaze was fixed on him, scarcely understanding. I was conscious that Dorothy had stopped, and was looking at me inquiringly.

'You are in a dream,' she said, and laughed. She turned her head and followed the direction of my eyes. Philip rose suddenly to his full height and sprang upon her playfully. She gave a piteous cry and shrank back—back from both of us; her eyes moved with a terrible look of fear from him to me, from me to him.

'Dolly, Dolly,' he cried, 'what's the matter? Have I startled you too much? I'm so sorry!'

I can scarcely say I had any feeling, now, but the one—a numb, dull pain throughout my body. I kept my eyes on her, but I was only vaguely conscious of my actions. I know I had the knife which I had used for the flowers, full open in my palm, and was pressing my fingers fiercely upon it ; the blood was trickling from my hands. I said no word. She looked at me, her face white and startled.

' Dolly, Dolly ! ' cried Philip in distress. ' Dick, what is this ? What are you doing here ? How came you here ? '

I still made no answer ; and then she spoke. ' Is it true ? ' she said in a low, fierce voice. ' Is it true ? You are not Philip ? '

I laughed.

' Philip ? ' I answered. ' No, not Philip, only his brother, who has the misfortune to be his double.'

She trembled like a reed.

' O you coward ! ' she cried ; ' you coward ! '

I clenched my hand ; the blood gushed from my fingers. Turning upon my heel I walked slowly down the pathway to the gate. As I lifted the latch I looked back and saw that she had fallen upon the sward, and that Philip was bending over her caressingly.

AKBAR ALI'S COURTYARD

HER head was bent as if in deep reflection, and for the moment I wondered if my eyes had played a trick upon me. But as she passed me for the third time she repeated the mute signal, and I turned and looked after her. When she had reached the corner she stopped, held up her hand, and beckoned. My doubts dispelled with the flash of that white arm, I started after her at a leisurely pace. Here, then, out of the wonderful night, and in this silent city, was some adventure quite to my liking. The thought of my inn fled forthwith, and though the hour was now late I felt my spirit rise freshly at this promise of romance. The lights were twinkling faintly in heaven, and in that soft gloaming I could see her white robes flitting before me in the dusk. So set was I in speculation upon the drift of my strange encounter that I did not particularly remark the direction of our course. It ran through narrow streets unknown to me, and into the hinder parts of the city, where the sultry air hung a little cooler, owing, doubtless, to the neighbourhood of the bay, which here cut the town in a heavy jag. Once or twice my guide, as I could perceive, glanced over her shoulder as though to discover if I were still pursuing; but in the main we continued as we had set forth—at a respectable distance, and with a feint of independence. At length, in some quiet street, she halted before a massive gate which seemed to give access to a large and handsome house. But even so I had no speech with her, for as I hurried forward to inquire my mission she disappeared into the darkness of the open gateway, and I caught but a flying glimpse of her. I should have gained little, it appeared, by a closer view, for she was heavily veiled; but at least I had seen she was of a lithe and youthful figure.

At the door I stood for a second irresolute. The suspicion that I had been misguided into a common intrigue rose frankly in my mind, but the next moment I discharged it and plunged into the blackness of the entrance. A passage of some sort, along which I groped, led into a spacious room lighted very partially by a swinging lamp. My guide had vanished, and I was the solitary tenant of a magnificent chamber. It was well-nigh bare of furniture, but most handsomely designed and decorated. Though the light was shed so faintly I could still make out the noble proportions of the pillars which sustained the ceiling, and were carven into strange erotic figures. Somewhere from the mistiness beyond I caught the plash of falling water, and a pleasant coolness pervaded the atmosphere. The floor, which was bare save for a square of carpet in the centre, was of mosaic work in red and silver, and seemed to my eyes prodigiously fine. The whole aspect of the place was witness to an owner of extreme wealth.

I had waited some time, impatient after my observations were over, but still a good deal curious, when a noise of slippered feet fell softly on my ears. Was it, I wondered, my fair guide returning to explain her odd invitation? A moment more, and I was disappointed by the entrance through the pillared corridor of an old man, dressed in the loose robe worn by the better

L

classes in those parts. He advanced to the patch of carpet, made me a low bow, and squatted carefully upon the floor, motioning me to do likewise. I obeyed his gesture, crossing my legs as comfortably as I was able after his own fashion, and we regarded each other for a while in silence. Then suddenly he clapped his hands, and at the sound there entered a tall black with coffee and narghiles, which he placed upon two dwarf tables at our elbows. When he had withdrawn, the old man, with another salaam of extreme courtesy, handed me a pipe, and by his example invited me to the coffee. We smoked and sipped without a word. This entertainment lasted but a brief time—briefer, indeed, than accords with the customs of the country. It was plain he was in haste, and (I judged) equally plain he had something upon his mind. For all his dignity he looked troubled, and a nervous twitching showed upon his face ; his hand trembled as he lifted his cup.

'I think, sir,' said I at last, 'you owe me some explanation of this visit. I was conducted to your door by an emissary from your household, and am here awaiting your pleasure.'

He laid his pipe upon the table and stroked his white beard.

'Sir,' said he, 'you are a stranger in this city, and a Giaour, but you are known to the faithful. I, at least, my son, have heard of you in the bazaars. You are wise; I am foolish. When a disease arises you go forth and destroy it with your arts. I, my son,' he said mournfully, 'I shut up my house and bow my head.'

'There is some one ill?' I asked, my romance flitting like a dream o' nights.

He assented with a gesture.

'Ill!' he exclaimed; 'ah, smitten with a thousand devils! I cannot keep silence. The light of my eyes is fading. My dove, the apple of my heart, is in the grip of a mortal disease. How can I bow my head to Allah, my son?'

He leaned his face upon his hands, and his frail old body shook with emotion. The sight of such a demonstration in one of so impassive a race and so resigned a creed stirred my surprise. I think he noticed it, for when he lifted his head again he took a puff at his pipe and resumed more calmly.

'You will wonder, my son,' he continued, 'that I, who am of the faithful, should intrust you, a Giaour, with my secret grief. But it is the will of Allah. I dreamed a dream. Allah is good. It shall be as he wills it.'

I made a movement to rise, and be done with what seemed merely a duty of my lost profession.

'Allah's will be done,' I said; 'if it be urgent, let me see this sick man.'

He raised his hand as though to deprecate my haste; his anxiety had made him prompt, but it was still the promptness of the Oriental only.

'Listen, my son,' he said. 'I am a merchant of this city, Akbar Ali by name, and a faithful servant of our Prophet, whose name be blessed. From my youth up I have lived among riches, and behold, if wealth can buy back my beloved from death I will pour out my gold as water.' He leaned forward to me; his face stiffened; suspicion, cunning, and greed lurked in his eyes. 'The presence of the Giaour in my household and among my women is a taint for ever; but this, too, shall be as Allah wills. You shall see her stretched upon the couch, veiled, and sleeping to her death. This shall you do in the presence of my slaves, who will bear me a report of all things. Go now, I beseech you, and heal her.'

He clapped his hands three times, and the black stole noiselessly out of the twilight. To him the merchant spoke in an undertone, and the slave with a bow begged me to follow him. From the corridor we passed into a large court-yard, open to the sky, and thence into a passage through the left wing of the house. Presently we arrived at a small antechamber, in which the black threw off his slippers, and whence, with his finger at his lips as for silence, he passed into a lofty room that overlooked part of the courtyard. It was lighted, as the other had been, by a swinging lamp, and was fur-nished luxuriously. Innumerable signs be-trayed the sex of its inhabitant, and had these been wanting, the prime fact lay there and stared me in the face. The couch upon which she was recumbent was very richly embroidered, like all else in the room, and at our entrance she made no movement, but remained supine and with a certain rigidity beneath her wrap-pings. The lamp illumined her fully, and I could perceive the bosom heaving slowly, but of face or body nought was visible. Save this indication of life it might have been some profusion of fine garments upon which I was gazing.

'This will never do,' said I to myself; and forthwith turned on the black. 'You must remove these coverings,' I said.

He looked at me quickly, salaamed, and stamped smartly on the floor. In an instant from everywhere about the room, as it seemed to me, issued a stream of women, all veiled and mute, who approached the couch like spectres. As my eyes went round the circle they lighted upon one a little apart from her fellows, whose slender body and gracious bearing I thought I recognised for those of my fair guide in the streets. I pointed to the couch.

'Let me see the face of your mistress,' said I.

There was a faint murmur from the bevy, but I repeated my request with authority.

'Would you have the Light of your master's life go out?' I said. 'Remove the veil. It is I that hold the keys of her life. These be my orders.'

At that one came stealthily forward and withdrew the heavy veil from before the face of my patient. Instantly a melancholy wail went round the waiting maidens. I stooped and looked into two shining eyes, black and lustrous as a night of stars. The face was beautiful, but pallid, and the jaw was tightly clenched; the lashes rose stirless, as the eyes stared into mine. A little shiver sprang up at the shoulders, and I traced its course through the drapery downwards along the contour of her body. I turned to the group of girls, some of whom, in their excitement, had discarded their veils.

'What is this sickness of your mistress?' I asked.

Then broke out at once a soft babble of liquid sounds, as one and all, with the incoherence of their kind, made answer together. The multitude of those silver voices rained confusion upon me, and with an impatient gesture I bade them begone. They vanished, I know not how, through the silken hangings about the walls, but as the last was flitting after her companions I stopped her. She turned to me. The face was still shrouded, but the whole aspect of the draped figure was familiar. I felt sure this was my stranger of the streets.

'Come,' said I, 'little one, tell me of this sickness.'

She stood near by the couch from which those prostrate eyes were still fixed upon me, and her soft voice rang very sweetly in my ears.

'Sir,' said she, 'I am a maid from the distant mountains, and have little knowledge. But the wife of my lord, my mistress, has been stricken sorely these many weeks. Day by day she lies upon the couch as you now see her, neither eating nor drinking, only staring with wide eyes. Night by night do the devils take her out into the courtyard, where she wanders alone in her madness. Nothing avails against the evil. Alas! the rose of the garden is fading away.'

She wrung her hands and appeared to weep behind her veil; and, shooting an accidental glance at the pale face on the pillows, I caught a gleam of the white teeth, a flash of the black eyes, and (I thought) a tiny smile, something mocking and malevolent. I bent down and examined my patient carefully. If here was madness there were a few symptoms patent now; if here was an somnambulist or a cataleptic she showed no visible sign of ailment. Indeed, one thing was plain from my scrutiny, that Akbar Ali must look deeper for the mystery than any physical ill ; for I would be sworn that I recognised every appearance of imposture in my invalid. The body was warm with generous life, the pulse as full as that of a healthy child, and the breath flowed naturally, with no trace of discomfort ; of malady there was not the slightest evidence. The girl covered up the face, and I left the chamber in wonder. I think I was relieved to find that my adventure was to exact more of me than a mere professional attendance. When I sought Akbar's presence I had resolved what conduct to adopt in this case. I would not throw it up as outside my skill ; indeed, I was already very curious and anxious at all hazards to pursue my inquiry to any end. And had there been any doubt in my mind as to my proper behaviour, Akbar himself would have confirmed my determination. I did but hint the illness was trifling and might not require my services, when he sprang into a passion of entreaty that I should stay and relieve it, cried that his pearl was slipping from him ; and, when I still seemed to hesitate, conducted himself as a man frantic with gloomy fears, offering me the utmost reward I should name. It was certain that he was utterly devoted to his wife ; certain, also, that he had been thoroughly frightened by her feint of insanity.

'Well,' said I, as though with reluctance, 'I will undertake her cure upon two conditions—my orders must be obeyed, and I must be free of the house.'

He accepted the terms with an alacrity from which I might estimate his anxiety. It was a very barbarous and novel experiment to place a Giaour in practical control of his household, but he was willing to go any length in the moment of his terror.

'Then,' said I, 'my first demand is a room to myself. Give me a chamber to which I shall have access day and night.'

He summoned the black and gave him some instructions, and I found myself at once in the possession of a comfortable apartment overlooking the courtyard, and in the wing of the buildings remote from the quarters of the women.

Next day I visited my mock-patient again,

and was the more convinced of her imposture. She was as well as I was myself, and far healthier than the shaking old man, her lord and master. She was, beyond question, an exceedingly handsome woman, young and vigorous, and if ever I saw passion in any eyes, it was in hers as she lay supine and seemingly unconscious, staring up into my face with great round orbs, impudent and unashamed. I could almost think that she enjoyed the novelty of thus confronting the Feringhi with her naked face. Her maid—for it was my graceful guide that waited upon us—declared she took no food; but this idea was preposterous, and I was pretty sure she had an excellent appetite, and ate like a healthy human being. I had no doubt but that there was some sort of conspiracy among her women to hoodwink the husband, but the reason for it I had yet to discover. My resolution to solve the problem was heightened by an incident that befell after I had left the room. For I was no sooner in the courtyard than I was attracted by the noise of a falling stool, and, glancing quickly back, I caught one glimpse of two black mocking eyes as they vanished from the window behind me.

In the evening I visited the house again, and took up my quarters in my private chamber. A little later I perceived the girl from the mountains drawing water in the courtyard, and I strolled out and met her. Her veil irritated me, for it pleased me to fancy that behind its soft meshes was hidden a face as beautiful as her gait and figure. One may fall in love with well-nigh any attribute of a woman, provided the others make no interference, and I have often been charmed by some miracle of moving grace, until a sudden turn of the head has thrown the features into view, and the picture has fallen into ill proportions. But of Zuleika (for such I found was her name), who kept her plainness or her beauty private, I had no thoughts but were pleasant and romantic. Her eyes, which were deep brown, peeped over the silk at me, but gave no clue to the rest of her features. She was from a remote part of the country, and came of a house of chieftains; but, having fallen into the hands of brigands in some raid upon her father's village, had passed into slavery, an orphan of very tender years. She had subsequently been purchased by Akbar to gratify Sulima—my patient, as it

appeared—whose caprice it was to have about
her person one of noble birth. She was com-
municative enough about her own fortunes, which
she related in her sweet, soft voice; but when
I questioned her as to her mistress she was at
once overtaken by agitation and embarrassment. If she did not actually know Sulima's
secret (which I suspected), she had clearly an
inkling of it, but with the fidelity of her calling
she kept her suspicions to herself, repeating her
original tale of lamentable illness. And that—
in its superficial facts at least—the story was
true I had proof that night. Somewhere about
nine o'clock, and in the midst of a great silence,
there sprang up a loud wailing in the courtyard. Hurrying out, I saw, under the light of
the rising moon, the figure of a woman march-
ing round the square and beating her breasts
with her hands. Scattered about at a little
distance stood a number of other figures, that
wept and wrung their hands, and called upon
Allah to rid their mistress, the Queen of
Beauty, of this sevenfold devil that was robbing
her of sense and life. As I watched her
curiously from the doorway I felt a grip upon
my arm, and the stricken face of old Akbar

appeared at my shoulder. He was trembling with alarm.

'Do you see?' he cried excitedly, 'the devils are killing her. My pearl, my pearl! Mahmoud, deliver us! Sir, this is what, under Allah's mercy, you shall cure. Ten thousand fortunes shall be yours if you will lay these devils.'

I gave him some words of comfort and dismissed him to his room.

'I will give myself a week,' I said, 'in which to destroy the devils. If at the end of that time she has still the malady, you may rank me as a common charlatan.'

He was quieted by my confidence, and tottered off muttering prayers and curses in alternation.

Soon the wailing died away, and the figure sank upon the stones of the courtyard, which seemed a signal for the disappearance of the maidens. They vanished simultaneously, and Sulima, her head bowed upon the flags, alone remained under the moon. Presently she rose, and walking vacantly, melted into the darkness of the women's wing. I hastened across the courtyard, but she was already gone; and silence once more pervaded the house.

'Here,' I thought, 'begins the mystery, and this must be my point of departure for its solution.'

The next day was appallingly hot; the sun struck into the white courtyard with the glare of a tiger, and the house of Akbar Ali was wrapt in slumber. No one ventured out, and after a perfunctory visit to Sulima I myself yielded to the languor of the air and took a noontide siesta. But later in the afternoon I threw off my lethargy and went out into the open. It seemed to me that now, if ever, was my chance of exploration; when no one was about to interfere with me, or to spy upon my actions. I entered the quarters of the women, and wandered through the rooms unchallenged. Now and then a prostrate figure upon a couch met my eye, but the place was singularly dead, and my slippered feet made no noise sufficient to arouse the dreamers. In my round I made but one discovery, and for that I forgave Sulima all my tedious hours of waiting. In one of the chambers I came upon the sleeping form of Zuleika, and she was unveiled. At the first sight of her face I fell back astonished, and then made an eager movement as though at

once to take possession of it. I think it was
the loveliest God has ever designed for poor
humanity; certainly it outstripped the creations
of my nimble imagination as much as those
had hitherto surpassed my experience. I had
never dreamed of such a face, so perfectly
fashioned, so exquisitely coloured, so soft and
radiant with beauty. In an instant it shot
home into my heart, and I have the picture of
that prostrate loveliness to-day as clear as the
reality of that enchanted moment. Passion
broke boisterously into my soul, and my blood
went leaping through my body as though I
had suddenly been transfigured by some divine
glory; the exhilaration of the feeling was like
nothing else on earth. I was drawn down to
that recumbent face with an attraction well-
nigh irresistible. I thank Heaven I stopped
short of the sacrilege in my thoughts. Instead,
I wrenched myself away and remained gazing
upon her from a distance; and then, with a
quick inspiration, tearing the golden ring from
my finger, I stealthily slipped it upon her left
hand. It was an impudent action, but I declare
I had no thought of liberty, much less of insult.
It was almost with childish glee that I noted

the effect of the transference, and then, fearing
lest better counsel should prevail over my impulse, I fled precipitately from the room.

That evening Sulima went through her performance in the courtyard as before, and, as
before, retired into the blackness of the passages
beyond. This time I was upon the alert, and
followed almost at her heels; but, in spite of
my precautions, I lost her somewhere in those
intricate and gloomy mazes. She vanished
soundlessly, and I was left to grope my way as
best I might back through the ill-lit rooms into
the freer air of the night. I was chagrined at
my failure, and saw plainly that I must take a
more heroic way with my impostor.

All the next day I saw no sign of Zuleika;
hour after hour I sat watching the courtyard
from my couch; but she did not appear, and
when, restless and ill at ease (for it was come to
that), I paid two visits to Sulima in the hope
of finding her, my mission was still fruitless—
another maid attended on her mistress. By the
evening I gave up in despair, and turned my
thoughts sadly upon the construction of a plot
to track the mock-invalid.

As was his custom, the black brought me

M

some coffee at the fall of night, set it upon the inlaid stool by my couch, and retired with a salaam. For some time I smoked in peace, revolving my plan. The lamp had remained unlit, and the room was now tolerably obscure, but the stool rose out of the gloom, a dim lump of whiteness. As I meditated I must have closed my eyes, and fallen drowsy, for suddenly I was startled by a soft sound as of breathing at my elbow, and this was followed immediately by a slight crash. I was up in a moment, and as I rose a white-clad figure melted softly into the mysteries about the doorway. The chamber was profoundly silent. I got off my couch, lit my lamp, and found my cup upset, and my coffee spilt to the dregs. To this I paid little heed, for my glance passed at once from the disaster to a ring that lay beside the sprawling cup upon the stool. It was that which I had so audaciously bestowed upon Zuleika's finger. A pang shot through me, for I perceived that my gift had been rejected, my overtures had been denied, and my hopes were broken. By this return I was taught a lesson in manners; she had put me in my proper place; her loveliness was not for me, and I must know it from the outset. These dismal reflections occupied me for some while, and the picture of Zuleika, as I had seen her in her sleep, stabbed me as it had been a knife. A sort of vague bitterness seized upon me. The East would have nothing to do with the West.

'At least,' I said, with a moody attempt at nonchalance, 'at least I'm not to be cheated of my coffee'; and forthwith I clapped my hands for the black.

He entered, and at sight of me I thought he started. I pointed to the overturned cup, from which the liquid was dripping to the floor. Instantly he had a fit of trembling, and fell upon his knees, praying for his life and pro-testing his innocence. It was his order, he explained with chattering teeth. For a moment I was puzzled at the exhibition of genuine terror, and then, enlightened by a quick sus-picion, I stooped and examined the dregs of the coffee. The lees were shot with horrid green streaks. Whether it had been poisoned or merely drugged, I never knew, but at once I understood the significance of the design.

'This is your mistress's work!' I said sternly.

'Dog, I will have you sliced in pieces and dropped into the bay for sharks to eat!'

He still asserted his innocence with manifest alarm.

'You shall learn,' I continued, 'that I am not to be trifled with. Bring me another cup.'

He obeyed with alacrity, and on his return I took it from his hands.

'Drink,' I said; 'drink, dog from the deserts, or I will force it down your throat.'

He sipped the coffee without hesitation, and, a look in his face convincing me, I snatched it from him and drained it at a draught.

'And now,' I continued, 'you shall await my return in security, monkeyface.'

He eyed me fearfully as I bound his hands with my handkerchief, but was in too great a state of trepidation to resist. Taking a curved dagger from the wall, I passed out and secured the door behind me. I was now on the eve of my adventure. On this night it was clear that Sulima was to undertake whatever enterprise she had in her mind, and (as she imagined) she would be free of the Giaour's eyes. I waited on the threshold of the corridor that communicated with the courtyard.

It was not long ere I perceived her issue from her room into the square. She went through her counterfeit of madness with her customary skill, but as it was not played for my benefit, the act was briefer than usual. Then she made off towards the lower part of the yard, and I followed stealthily in the shadows. Having no fear of pursuit, she went leisurely enough, and I found no difficulty in keeping her in sight. We entered a dark doorway, traversed a succession of passages noiselessly, and presently came into a small room, barely lighted, in the centre of which she halted and stooped to the floor. I shrank into the hangings about the entrance and watched her. She put her face well-nigh to the stone, and murmured softly—

'Little slave,' she said, 'open! It is the Star of Evening.'

At the words a thin rumble fell on my ear, a slab of stone slid gently back, and a gap yawned slowly in the floor. Into this Sulima descended, and as her head sank below the level of the hole, the stone leisurely stole out of its socket and crept over the aperture. It was the crisis of my adventure. Should that lid close upon the crevice, I was shut off for ever from my quarry, and must needs retreat impotently to my bed. I took the decision in a moment, and stepping lightly forward thrust the tip of my dagger into the vanishing slit. The stone met the steel and rested, and to my joy there was no click of a latch. Thus I stood impatiently for some minutes, in fear lest my action had been detected ; but as nothing happened I bent low, and, inserting my fingers in the crack, pulled at the lid with all my strength. Gradually it yielded, and, sliding with a soft, grating sound, disclosed a square black patch of space. After a momentary hesitation I dropped my feet into this and hit upon a ledge, which proved to be the topmost step in a stone stairway. I descended quietly, and at the bottom of the flight found myself in a passage of some sort. Along this I felt my way until at length I burst out into a lighted corridor, supported on either side by pillars. When I had reached the end of this, I stumbled upon another staircase which curved upwards and finished before a heavy curtain. And here, cautiously peering through a chink, I perceived that I was on the threshold of a large chamber. It was quite bare and untenanted, and at the further side another curtained doorway gave entrance to a small and very dark antechamber. When I had got so far I could hear from somewhere in the darkness the sound of murmuring voices, and towards these I groped my way. I now discovered that the antechamber was but an alcove to a more spacious room from which it was shut off by a mass of silken hangings. Through these I peeped, and my eyes alighted· on Sulima.

The secret was out at last. The room before me was daintily furnished, after a sensuous Oriental fashion, and upon one of the couches in the centre sat my patient, clinging about her lover's neck. He was a young man, tall and dark, and, to judge by his face, of fierce emotions. This was striking enough, and even handsome after a barbaric pattern. A jewelled sword hung by his side, and he seemed from his dress and his bearing to be a soldier—indeed, one of high authority at the Court, I guessed. He caressed her with many endearments, and I think I never saw a greater abandonment to passion marked upon any woman's face. She was whispering softly in his ear, but not so softly that I could not catch something of her speech.

'They set a watch upon me, beloved,' she murmured, 'but I was strong in my love; I was not to be chained. The Evening Star shall rise whatever be their poor tricks. O my beloved, I love thee!'

Her cooing grew too inarticulate for my ears, and presently she broke into a melodious laugh.

'I have cheated them, heart of me. The fool, my husband, is distraught with terrors for my health. He thinks me mad, and mad I am for love of thee. He set the Giaour to heal me; but the Giaour was wise and frowned upon me; and another moth is shrivelled and gone. Such and such is the fate of those that would cross me and my beloved!'

As I stood listening, I know not through what clumsiness of movement, my dagger dropped from my hand and clattered on the stone floor. The man seized his sword and jumped to his feet, and Sulima, with a cry of alarm, clung to his arm. And then, in recovering my weapon, I must needs tread awkwardly upon the curtain, and, tripping myself, fall heavily to my knees. Instantly the man ran forward with his raised weapon, while Sulima, terror in her eyes, burst through the hangings with a shriek,

and, rushing across the antechamber, fled out
of sight. I had scarce time to notice this out
of the tail of my eye when my enemy was
upon me. I stepped back into the darkness, and
saw him break through the curtain. I heard
his sword singing as he swept it blindly about
him, and then a clamp of feet made for me. I
cannot tell by what miracle his weapon missed
me ; it is possible he had no notion of my
position, and was merely coming at a venture ;
for the curtains had fallen to, and the alcove
was pitch dark. Even so it is a mystery that I
should have escaped the circles of his sword.
But the bare fact is that as I instinctively held
my dagger at arm's-length before me, by way
of protection, he ran upon it. I had a sudden
shock as his body struck the point, and then
felt something give ; a slight groan followed,
the weapon was jerked from my hand, and there
was the dull sound of a falling body. The
affair was over in a moment, and with little
noise ; and I stood by the side of the dead
man, bewildered and unnerved. I must have
remained thus for some minutes, for I was
aroused from my stupefaction by a whisper out
of the surrounding quiet.

'You must go at once,' it said. 'Mustapha is awaking from his sleep. What is this you have done? Oh! you will be slain! you will be slain!'

The voice trembled with tears, and though I could make out nothing in the darkness, I recognised it in an instant for Zuleika's. I put out my hands, and, happening upon her, drew her into the lighted room beyond.

'How did you come here?' I asked. 'What is this place?'

Her lovely face, frightened and wonderstruck as it was, dropped suddenly upon her bosom.

'What is this place?' I repeated. She raised her head quickly and looked at me tearfully; she put an arm towards me in the utmost agitation.

'You must go,' she cried; 'you will be killed, and I——.' She put her hands to her face and wept.

A strong emotion surged through me. I took her hand again.

'I will not go,' I said, 'until you have answered my questions. Why are you here?'

'I came,' she whispered, 'to warn you. I watched you enter the pit; I followed you. I have been at your heels all the way.'

I was illumined by a flash of intelligence.

'And the coffee,' I asked breathlessly, 'what of that?'

She made no answer.

'It was you saved me, then,' I continued. 'You knew. Alas! dear one, why did you return me the ring? Of what use is my life without you? My beloved, why are you here?'

I drew her towards me; she looked up with her wide and shining eyes.

'Give it me back,' she murmured. 'I left it for a sign. Give it back to me.'

In an ecstasy at her unexpected words I slipped it off my finger upon hers, and put my arms about her. She clung close, and I kissed her from my soul. Upon the very spot which a few moments before had been the scene of the illicit passions of Sulima and the hapless dead, there we exchanged the mutual ardours of our pure affection.

'My beloved,' I said, 'light of my life, my pearl, I love you!'

Zuleika sighed, and then hastily withdrew herself from me.

'But you must go,' she cried; 'my heart beats a warning. I hear the voice of my own heart talking. O my beloved, and my lord, you must fly! Mustapha is at the door, and, behold, the sleep is lifting from his eyelids. Come.'

I followed her to the doorway of the big chamber that led upon the stairway.

'Hush!' she whispered, pointing with her finger; and there, upon the very margin of the room, squat against the curtain that defended the stairway, I perceived what seemed to me at the first glance a monstrous toad.

'It is Mustapha,' she explained, 'step lightly.' And, sure enough, when we reached the object, which was rolling uneasily in its slumber, and breathing stertorously, my eyes fell on the most horrid and grotesque black dwarf that may be conceived. It lay in a misshapen lump, like nothing earthly, and its hideous appearance, together with the ugly noises it was making, made me shudder and shrink as from a species of devil. As we passed, its heavy-lidded eyes, sodden with opium or hasheesh, fell open and stared at us without intelligence. Once in the corridor, I breathed without alarm, and we began to move between the pillars by the aid of the dim light. I now saw that the place we were traversing extended much further upon

either side than I had previously imagined.
Indeed, it seemed to be a vault of considerable
dimensions, and the columns that supported
it ran off into the darkness of the remoter
parts, from which they peeped like a row of
stationary ghosts.

When we had got about halfway along this
Zuleika halted, and put her hand out to detain
me.

'There is something beyond,' she whispered.
'Rest, beloved, and I will go forward.'

I protested against this rashness, but she
enjoined upon me silence, murmuring, 'I have
no fears. I am safe, jewel of my eyes. Here I
have freedom to come and go.'

She left me, fading imperceptibly from my
eyes, and I waited, a prey to anxiety. The
sound of a low voice reached me from the
distance, a tiny cry followed; and in high
agitation I ran forward, fearing for her safety.
But at that moment a form glided into view,
and I stepped swiftly to it. I seized her hand.

'Zuleika,' I said.

Instantly the figure started back, trembling
under my touch; and, looking closer, I saw
that I had hold of Sulima. She winced from

me as from a spirit ; evidently she had thought
me drugged or dead long since.

'The game is played out, my pretty mad-
woman,' I said sternly. 'Pray allow me to
conduct you to your husband's house.'

She stared at me, and at last spoke.

'So you have tracked me then, spy of a
Giaour,' she said scornfully. 'It is a generous
trade, this of yours. And now fly to your
master and obtain your reward.'

I tightened my grasp upon her.

'I at least have not deceived a fond old
husband,' I answered. 'Go you, and Allah
pardon you, for this is the end of your trickery.'

She examined me attentively for a few
seconds.

'You will tell him all?' she said. 'There is
the sack and the bay for me,' and she laughed
bitterly ; but in a moment changed her tone,
and, clasping my arm, fell into the most piteous
entreaties. 'Let me go,' she pleaded, 'O
Giaour, let me go. Hadst thou never a lover ?
Dost thou know what passion may be ? Thou
wouldst tie me to this silly dotard, with a brave
and noble lover waiting at my gate ? And
thou thyself hast felt the pangs of love ! Ah !

let me go! Return to thy country; turn thy feet free of this city, and leave him to his illusions and me to my happiness.'

'I have no intention of betraying you,' I replied. 'That is for the spy, with whom you have compared me. But this sham is at an end.'

She looked at me craftily.

'I swear it,' she said; 'it is at an end if you will keep my secret. O wise and faithful! I swear by our Prophet it shall end.'

I said nothing, for suddenly I remembered that she was in ignorance of the tragic conclusion of her intrigue, and that what she protested she would accomplish was already taken from her hands by the act of death.

'Come, then,' I said; 'let us leave this place.'

She obeyed me, and together we completed the remainder of the journey, and remounted the stairs to the lid of the pit. It was at this point that my thoughts flew to Zuleika. Where had she gone? Whither had she fled? Recalling the voices I had heard in the corridor, I turned to my companion.

'Where is Zuleika?' I asked abruptly. She gazed at me curiously, and then a smile danced in her eyes.

'Ah!' she said, 'you have, then, a heart. You will pity me; you will not condemn. It is to this I owe my pardon. O Giaour! I thank you.'

And, with a gleam of her liquid eyes, she was gone.

In the morning I had an interview with Akbar, who received me eagerly.

'Akbar Ali,' I said, 'last night did I accomplish the cure your heart desires. And look, here is the course this disease will run. This day once more will she lie prostrate among her weeping maidens; this night for the last time the devils will seize her in the courtyard. But they will then leave her. Two days she will shut herself up, refusing food, and lamenting with a great sorrow, till the weakness be past. But on the third day she will rise and go about the house as was her wont before the malady took her. And thus you shall be free of your fears.'

The man was quite overcome with this prospect, and displayed his joy in a way quite unprecedented in my Oriental experience. He shook my hand in both his own, and declared he was under the deepest debt of gratitude, called down the blessings of Allah and his

Prophet on my head, vowed he would intercede for me in Paradise, and wound up by offering me as much of his treasure as I should ask in payment for my services. I bade him keep calm, and part with nothing till my predictions should be fulfilled; and then, promising to return on the third day, left him, and set forth for my inn. I had hoped to see Zuleika before I went, but the disappointment fed the pleasures of anticipation. I should be three days without sight or touch of her, and for this denial the coming reunion would be all the sweeter. I had made up my mind long since what reward I would exact of the merchant, and during my voluntary absence from the house the thought of it kept me in the blithest temper. When I arrived on the appointed day Akbar Ali gave me an effusive welcome. My prophecy had come true, he said; Sulima was about her quarters, as of old; but she was in poor spirits, and had been very melancholy; her maids said she would weep bitterly in the night. I explained that this would pass, and she would return to him again; and Akbar, nothing doubting, drew me into the women's wing, and bade me peep through the curtains and behold my cure.

N

Sulima was sitting on her couch, her elbows on a little ivory table, gazing before her at the window. She turned at the sound of her husband's whisper, and looked towards the doorway. I think I have never seen a face so stricken with sorrow, so marked and delineated by utter grief. But the next second, as her eyes caught mine, the whole aspect changed ; a flash lit up her sad eyes, and every feature was transfigured with a malignant passion of cruelty and hate. I had no need to wonder if she knew.

I put my demands before the merchant without delay.

' I ask one little thing,' I said, 'and you have sworn by your Prophet that you will give me my price. Neither gold nor jewels do I want, but one thing only. Give me Zuleika, the little mountain maiden that waits upon your wife.'

He smiled all over his yellow face, and was disposed in his good temper to be even facetious. He stroked his beard and chuckled.

' Allah be my witness,' he answered. ' Yes, you shall have her. For, O Giaour ! there is but one way with Giaour or Believer, and that is a worthy way. You have given me back my wife. It is meet I should give you yours.'

He clapped his hands, still chuckling, and the black obeyed his summons.

'Bring me,' said he, 'the slave-girl, Zuleika.' The black hesitated. 'Quick,' he cried, 'or by the beard of the Prophet——'

The black salaamed low.

'Lord of our lives,' he answered, 'the girl is not here.'

I sprang to my feet, and the stool crashed upon the mosaic. The merchant lifted his hand.

'My son,' he said, 'be still.' And then to the black: 'Thief of a slave and dog of an alien pack, what is this story you bring me?'

The black bowed deeper.

'It is true, O Presence!' he muttered. 'The girl is gone. There is no trace of her within the gates of this house. She vanished two days ago.'

I stared at him, horrorstruck; my body trembled from head to foot. For at that instant I saw, not the impassive face of the black, nor Akbar's wrathful countenance, but the fierce flash of malignant hatred lighting up the eyes of Sulima.

THE sunlight streamed through the blue-gums on the slant, and lay in waving patches upon the carpet. The passion-flowers that mantled the verandah nodded in the little airs of eventide, and the many scents of the bush suffused the room. Frere eased his holland coat upon his shoulders, and threw a glance out of the open windows on the west.

'Mutton,' said he, 'is preposterous to-night, my dear.'

'I gave you your choice,' returned his wife playfully. 'Beef or mutton or pork—our three staples, Mr. Gray,' she added, turning to the young man on her left.

The cadet laughed.

'Cold roastbeef and salad,' he muttered.

'You're not in Paris, my boy,' said the squatter. 'Mayonnaise and such things belong to a different world than ours. There's plenty of food, but little variety here.'

196

'It's a comfort to have learnt you're not cannibals,' said the cadet. 'That's the prevalent opinion at home.'

The door creaked a little on its hinges, and the manager looked up then down again.

'No, we're civilised to a point,' responded Frere thoughtfully. 'The ladies will tell you this is an error, but it's a fact. Our barbarism takes only the form of monotony and hospitality. There's always a seat for a stranger in this country.'

'Glad to hear it.'

The door closed sharply; all turned swiftly from the table and beheld a man of middle height, with a short black beard, standing in the doorway. He was attired after the rough bush habit, and wore a wide felt hat on the back of his head. Frere started to his feet.

'What the devil——'

The breeze blowing in the trellis of the verandah opened a peep-hole for the dying sun, and a beam fell sharply upon a nozzle of steel. The squatter stopped and stared, and the cadet and the manager did likewise.

'I'm particularly peckish,' said the newcomer, 'and there's a vacant seat beside the missis. Reserved for an honoured guest, I s'pose,' he added with a grin; and playing ostentatiously with his weapon, he marched round the table with the long stride of one accustomed to the saddle.

'Who are you?' asked the cadet angrily, staring in astonishment from the man to the squatter, whose face had turned ashen. The manager pulled him down.

'For God's sake, sit still,' he whispered. 'It's Blackbeard.'

The man, overhearing the tragic whisper, grinned and nodded, 'A young man out from England, I s'pose. Mister, your servant,' and with his left hand he whipped his chair adroitly to the table. Mrs. Frere shrank away, and Gray made a sensible movement towards her. Blackbeard stuck his arm upright upon the board, and leaned his head upon the hand that held the revolver. Grabbing his plate with the other hand, he pushed it into the air with an extravagant gesture of bravado.

'Mutton'll suit me to a *t*,' he said. 'Frere, some mutton.'

The squatter's hands trembled a little; his eye wandered from the bushranger to his wife, and her sister, who was gazing with set eyes of horror at the intruding apparition. He laughed an uneasy laugh, and cut some meat.

'I didn't know you were in these parts,' he said nervously. 'They said you were up Moolara way.'

'Moolara's played out,' said the bushranger. 'But Frere's always good for a poor devil.'

He laid his weapon on the table, and seizing his knife and fork, began his meal. For some time there was silence, and then the man spoke again.

'You keep good sheep, Frere Esquire,' he said. 'Half-bred Leicester, ain't it? I thought I knew the breed.'

Frere made no answer, but looked expectantly at the door.

'Damn it, don't let's have an unsociable meal,' said the man in aggrieved tones. 'Speak up, Frere. You're good enough on the stump. The bully-faced Garrod never had a tongue.'

He leered at the manager, who mumbled in his beard. Frere looked at the door.

'I suppose you've managed this affair all right,' he said presently. 'The men——'

'Shut up in the barns, with Crusoe standing guard,' broke in Blackbeard. 'I ain't the sort to make a miss on the racket I've played so long, mate. Got 'em all in a corral, with Crusoe's lead to frighten 'em. My God,' he said, swelling in his swagger, 'I'd do any job of this sort in half an hour with a boy behind me. Crusoe and me's fit for a stationful.'

Frere said nothing, but still glanced at the door. The bushranger turned to the white girl on his right, and mincing with his face, bobbed his head.

'Charming weather,' he asserted. 'A trifle hot, but seasonable, seasonable.'

'Very hot,' said Frere, pulling the girl's chair towards him. 'Some more mutton?'

'Thank ye, Frere. As you press me——'

The cadet, who had been struck dumb with wonder and indignation, now made a movement, but the manager, fearful of an accident, put out his hand, and whispered, 'Don't move. One of the hands will be here directly. He's been over to Forsyth. If he comes up the long track Crusoe'll miss him. Frere's watching the door.'

'Now, young gimcrack, you've a voice,' said

the stranger suddenly; 'what's your sentiments?'

'You're the blackest-looking ruffian I've
seen in my day,' returned the cadet promptly.

Blackbeard laughed. 'It ain't exactly polite,'
he said. 'There's heaps worse than me. I'm
genteel in my own line, ain't I, ladies?'

He leered round the table, and Frere rose to
his feet.

'Good heavens, man,' he cried, 'let the ladies
leave the room, at any rate.'

'Sit down, Frere,' said the bushranger. 'Let
'em stop and see the play, you cruel chap.
It'll be over directly.'

Frere sat down.

'Well, well, let us go to business, then,' he
said impatiently. 'What do you want?'

Blackbeard sat back in his chair, and regarded his host carelessly.

'If I'd known you were so sensible, I'd have
been here long ago,' he said. 'I won't cut you
down for the sake of the dinner and the ladies,
but I'll take the blessed haul, minus ten per
cent, and a couple of horses, and the young
gimcrack's gold watch. I'm damn sure he's
got a gold watch—they all have when they

come out from England—and mine's gone
wrong.'

'Then take it and go,' said Frere, whose eyes
suddenly lighted up. A sound came in from
the verandah; Blackbeard made no movement,
but kept his keen eyes on his host, whose flurry
was now perceptible. The cadet turned, and
stared at the door, which creaked. The manager
eyed Blackbeard across the table. In another
moment there was a footstep, and the door
opened. Blackbeard did not rise. The new-
comer, a station hand, hot and dusty with travel,
broke into the room, then stopped with his eye
on the bushranger. There was a general movement. The new-comer backed to the half-open
door.

'Don't go, mate,' cried Blackbeard.

'Damn you, you're copped,' cried the hand
in answer, taking the doorway at a stride.

Blackbeard raised his hand. 'By God, you
don't,' he said. There was a crack of a revolver, and the man staggered and fell halfway
across the threshold.

'You accursed hound!' yelled the manager.
The ladies shrieked; Frere darted forward, and
in a moment Gray had his hands at the bush-

ranger's throat. The black barrel gleamed in his face, in which the sulphur still fumed, and he shrank away.

'Remember, gentlemen, there are ladies present,' said the bushranger sardonically. 'Sit down and go on grubbing.' He walked to the door, and bent over the fallen man. 'A bit of poultice 'll do him right enough, and I 'll look in on the road, and send a doctor from Moolara. Very sorry, matey, but there ain't afterthoughts in my profession.'

'Out, you black scoundrel!' said Frere fiercely.

'Going, going, boss,' returned he; 'but first you and I do this business together.'

Frere threw down a purse with a gesture of impatience. The bushranger scrutinised it and winked.

'I fancy I ain't come for this,' he said. 'Frere Esquire paid a visit to his bank last week, and said bank ain't empty. I ought to know the size of a cashbox when I see it by this time.'

He indicated a bureau at the bottom of the room. Frere laughed harshly.

'You 're mighty smart, Blackbeard. Why didn't you take to politics?'

'I would make a good Attorney-General, Frere, wouldn't I ? '

The squatter unlocked his bureau and took out an iron box. 'Take it and go,' he said irritably.

'Hold on a bit; my mount's a bit groggy, and I 'll take the liberty of borrowing a horse from you, Frere. Just you come along and help me choose him. I shall want a fast one to get this blamed doctor for you. There's two women,' he said, looking round, 'and a lame man. They can look after him. I 'll take—— No, sonny,' he said, with a grin at the cadet. ' Hang it, I ain't come to being scared of a new chum. Stop and take care of the women, sonny; we 'll manage the horses.' So saying, he took Frere's arm with one hand, and Garrod's with the other, and marched out between his unwilling attendants. The door shut to sharply.

As they vanished through the doorway there was a moment's silence, and then Gray stepped forward and pulled at the handle.

'Why, it's not locked,' he exclaimed in surprise.

'Oh, please don't go. Shut it again,' cried

Mrs. Frere anxiously. 'He'll do some more harm if you follow.'

'Yes, let him alone, and he'll go away quietly,' said her sister, who had bent down over the wounded man.

Gray stood in thought. The frank contempt of the bushranger for all new chums, as for something ignoble and ludicrous, rankled in his bosom.

'I can't let him go off like this,' he said at last. 'If I knew where there was a gun——'

'There's a revolver in the kitchen, Mr. Gray,' said the hand. 'Shoot the brute right away.'

'No, no,' said Mrs. Frere.

But Gray was already gone. The wounded pride of manhood smarted bitterly; and as he crossed the verandah and passed into the yard, he was resolved to prove himself the superior of this bragging bully. The hacks were loose in a paddock beyond the stables, and he knew that Blackbeard was taking his companions in that direction. But over a piece of kitchen-garden and along a line of young blue-gums, a shorter track led to the stables—of which it was not at all likely that the bushranger was aware. To pursue this was to cut him off, and come out in concealment ere he reached the paddock. He leapt over the little fence beyond a patch of cabbages, and struck off through the next paddock as fast as he might. Twenty yards further he crawled through the hedge of furze, and was in the open yards about the stables. He came out immediately at the back of a building, and, having no fear of being seen, and being anxious to arrive in time, he crept round the corner and dashed into a run. Halfway across the stable-yard a man hailed him suddenly.

'Say, mister, have you got a light?'

He stopped, and turning quickly in the direction of the sound, saw a mean-looking little man, clad in very foul corduroys, but otherwise after the ordinary fashion of the station hands. He had a broken cutty pipe in his mouth, and was stuffing down the black tobacco with his fingers as he approached the cadet.

'Lend me a match, mate,' he asked in a squeaky voice.

Gray, in the full swing of his breathless excitement, took him by the arm.

'Come on,' he said eagerly; 'come and give me a hand. There's a bushranger about.'

'Blackbeard?' queried the dirty little man.

'Yes, I'm on his trail; follow me.'

'Hold on! If it's Blackbeard, seems to me, matey, you'd better quit. He's a rare one, is Blackbeard. Taken much?'

Gray nodded, with his eyes roaming anxiously about the horizon.

'Who'll he have with him?' asked the stranger. 'Why, Crusoe, I s'pose.'

Gray nodded. 'Yes, yes; I believe so.'

'Well, better stop and get breath,' said the little man soothingly. 'Crusoe's a smart chap, too. I heard tell how he stuck up a place without a mate, and no more ammunition than an old gin-bottle. Oh, he's a smart chap.'

'Look here, my man,' said Gray impatiently, 'are you coming with me or not?'

'Not much,' was the answer, followed by a chuckle.

'Why, there they go,' said the cadet excitedly; 'see him moving down to that paddock with the white gate. I'll just be in time.'

'Not much, you fool,' said the squeaky voice. 'You just got to stay here and be friendly like.'

Gray turned slowly to his companion, struck mute with astonishment, and looked into the barrel of a revolver. Suddenly the truth flashed upon him. 'Crusoe!' he stammered.

'That's about it,' said the other complacently; 'and you're a new chum, I'll lay.'

'How infernally ignominious,' thought Gray, as he contemplated the pigmy figure of his gaoler.

'No go, guv'nor. Put down your 'ands.'

Gray bit his lips. 'What do you intend to do?' he asked.

'Nothin', Johnny, nothin'. Sit still, that's all. Me and Blackbeard don't like making a mess.'

'He's made a mess down at the house,' said Gray sharply.

'Oh, has he?' said Crusoe thoughtfully. 'Then I suppose we'll have to lay low a bit.'

As he spoke there was the report of a gun, and a bullet sang in Gray's ears.

'What the devil!' cried Crusoe, whipping round upon his prisoner; but Gray was staring towards the house in wonder.

'Oh, some one over there!' said Crusoe. 'Well, this looks like getting too hot for me; we'll go behind the stable.'

He seized Gray by the arm, but as he turned

threw up his hands suddenly and gasped. A loud report followed. The bushranger fell against the cadet, and slipped awkwardly to the ground in a heap. The cadet looked with curious terror on the body, and then back towards the house. The gorse on the hedge through which he had crept parted, and for a moment he saw the glint of a gun and the face of the wounded hand. He had hardly time to make the discovery when he heard the sound of voices behind him, and the footsteps of some people running drew nearer.

'Blackbeard,' he thought, and darting across the yard, crept into a patch of scrub which had not been cleared from before the stables. He was no sooner in hiding than the bushranger, with his two reluctant hosts, turned the corner and came into the yard.

'By God!' said Blackbeard, as his eyes fell on Crusoe's body, 'shot, and shot in the back.' He looked slowly round. 'To think it should be that new chum of yours, Frere. A long shot, a straight shot, and a damned shabby shot.'

Frere turned away with a movement of disgust.

'You'd better go,' he said. 'Here's more

bloodshed than I want to deal with. Take the horse and be off.'

Blackbeard said nothing, but handling his revolver, turned slowly round, scrutinised all the quarters of the yard. His eyes rested uneasily upon the patch of scrub.

'Going, Frere, going,' he said at last, and appeared to meditate. 'That cadet of yours is too good a shot, and I don't hold with scurvy fighting. I like to know where my man is.' His eyes returned to the scrub, and he backed behind Garrod. 'Look here, Frere,' he said at last, 'let's call a truce. We've bungled this business, and it's my fault. Let's set the clock back. You take the swag again, and give me a hundred paces. I don't like that shot in the back, and it's a fact. Make a bargain with me, and I'll trouble you to make it at the top of your voice, too.' As he spoke he raised his own fast voice, still with his eye on the scrub. 'Here's the gold again, and now you take your oath to let me go free from any darned sharp-shooter to the corner of the paddock. After that he may go to the devil.'

'I agree,' said Frere.

'Shake hands on it, mate,'

Blackbeard gripped the squatter firmly, and then ostentatiously stuck his revolver back into his belt, and with one final glance at the scrub, turned his back upon his companions and strode out of the yard. His way lay very close to the scrub, and as he passed it, a movement was discernible in the bushes.

'Lie down, man,' said Frere angrily. Blackbeard said nothing, but kept his eye on the spot and his hand on the weapon. Suddenly, and with a spring, Gray stood on the pathway before him. Bang went Blackbeard's revolver in a moment, and the next instant the new chum grappled with him. The two men wrestled together, and Frere, running up, heard Gray's voice shouting breathlessly and persistently, 'Surrender, you ruffian! Surrender, you ruffian!'

The struggle endured for some minutes, but neither man got any material advantage over the other, and then the bushranger suddenly flung himself clear of his adversary, and levelled his weapon. Gray fingered stupidly for his revolver, but could not find it. There was an instant's hesitation, and then he had rushed with lifted fist upon Blackbeard. As he did so the latter pulled his trigger, but the same moment there came a crack from Garrod's direction, and the bushranger fell over on his side. Gray stumbled and fell upon the prostrate man, who swore feebly.

'Who shot me?' he asked faintly. 'Bully-faced Garrod, by God! That was damned mean, too;' and his body shook and settled into silence.

Printed by T. and A. Constable, Printers to Her Majesty
at the Edinburgh University Press

John Lane

The Bodley Head

VIGO STREET, LONDON, W.

THE KEYNOTES SERIES.

Crown 8vo, cloth. Each volume with a Title-page and Cover Design by AUBREY BEARDSLEY. 3s. 6d. net.

Copyright Editions of the volumes of the KEYNOTES SERIES are published in the United States by Messrs. ROBERTS BROS. of Boston.

Sixth Edition, now ready.

KEYNOTES. By GEORGE EGERTON. With Title-page by AUBREY BEARDSLEY. Crown 8vo, cloth, 3s. 6d. net.

'Emboldened, doubtless, by the success of "Dodo," the author of "Keynotes" offers us a set of stories written with the least amount of literary skill and in the worst literary taste. We have refrained from quotation, for fear of giving to this book an importance which it does not merit.'—*Pall Mall Gazette.*

'The sirens sing in it from the first page to the last. It may, perhaps, shock you with disregard of conventionality and reticencies, but you will all the same have to admit its fascination. There can be no doubt that in Mr. George Egerton his publishers have discovered a story-teller of genius. —*Star.*

'This is a collection of eight of the prettiest short stories that have appeared for many a day. They turn for the most part on feminine traits of character; in fact, the book is a little psychological study of woman under various circumstances. The characters are so admirably drawn, and the scenes and landscapes are described with so much and so rare vividness, that one cannot help being almost spell-bound by their perusal.'—*St. James's Gazette.*

'A rich, passionate temperament vibrates through every line. . . . We have met nothing so lovely in its tenderness since Mr. Kipling's "Without Benefit of Clergy."'—*Daily Chronicle.*

'For any one who cares more for truth than for orthodox mummery, and for the real flood of the human heart than for the tepid negus which stirs the veins of respectability, this little book deserves a hearty welcome.' —*Sketch.*

'Singularly artistic in its brilliant suggestiveness.'—*Daily News.*

'This is a book which is a portentous sign of our times. The wildness, the fierceness, the animality that underlie the soft, smooth surface of woman's pretty and subdued face—this is the theme to which she again and again recurs.'—T. P. in *Weekly Sun.*

'To credit a new writer with the possession of genius is a serious matter, but it is nevertheless a verdict which Mr. George Egerton can hardly avoid at the hands of those who read his delightful sketches.'—*Liverpool Post.*

'These lovely sketches are informed by such throbbing feeling, such insight into complex woman, that we with all speed and warmth advise those who are in search of splendid literature to procure "Keynotes" without delay.'—*Literary World.*

'These very clever stories of Mr. Egerton's.'—*Black and White.*

'The reading of it is an adventure, and, once begun, it is hard to tear yourself from the book till you have devoured every line. There is impulsive life in every word of it. It has passion, ardour, vehement romance. It is full of youth; often enough the revolt and despair of youth.'—*Irish Independent.*

'Every line of the book gives the impression that here some woman has crystallised her life's drama; has written down her soul upon the page. —*Review of Reviews.*

'The work of a woman who has lived every hour of her life, be she young or old. . . . She allows us, like the great artists of old, Shakespeare and Goethe, to draw our own moral from the stories she tells, and it is with no uncertain touch or faltering hand that she pulls aside the curtain of conventional hypocrisy which hundreds of women hang between the world and their own hearts. . . . The insight of the writer into the curious and complicated nature of women is almost miraculous.'—*Lady's Pictorial.*

'Not since the "Story of an African Farm" was written has any woman delivered herself of so strong, so forcible a book.'—*Queen.*

'She is a writer with a profound understanding of the human heart. She understands men; and, more than this, she understands women. . . . For those who weary of the conventional fiction, and who long for something out of the ordinary run of things, these are tales that carry the zest of living.'—*Boston Beacon.*

'It is not a book for babes and sucklings, since it cuts deep into rather dangerous soil; but it is refined and skilful . . . strikes a very true and touching note of pathos.'—*Westminster Gazette.*

'The author of these able word sketches is manifestly a close observer of Nature's moods, and one, moreover, who carefully takes stock of the up-to-date thoughts that shake mankind.'—*Daily Telegraph.*

'Powerful pictures of human beings living to-day, full of burning pain, and thought, and passion.'—*Bookman.*

'A work of genius. There is upon the whole thing a stamp of down-right inevitableness as of things which must be written, and written exactly in that way.'—*Speaker.*

'"Keynotes" is a singularly clever book.'—*Truth.*

THE DANCING FAUN. By FLORENCE FARR. With Title-page and Cover Design by AUBREY BEARDSLEY. Crown 8vo, 3s. 6d. net.

'We welcome the light and merry pen of Miss Farr as one of the deftest that has been wielded in the style of to-day. She has written the cleverest and the most cynical sensation story of the season.'—*Liverpool Daily Post.*

'Slight as it is, the story is, in its way, strong.'—*Literary World.*

'Full of bright paradox, and paradox which is no mere topsy-turvy play upon words, but the product of serious thinking upon life. One of the cleverest of recent novels.'—*Star.*

'It is full of epigrammatic effects, and it has a certain thread of pathos calculated to win our sympathy.'—*Queen.*

'The story is subtle and psychological after the fashion of modern psychology; it is undeniably clever and smartly written.'—*Gentlewoman.*

'No one can deny its freshness and wit. Indeed there are things in it here and there which John Oliver Hobbes herself might have signed without loss of reputation.'—*Woman.*

'There is a lurid power in the very unreality of the story. One does not quite understand how Lady Geraldine worked herself up to shooting her lover, but when she has done it, the description of what passes through her mind is magnificent.'—*Athenæum.*

'Written by an obviously clever woman.'—*Black and White.*

'Miss Farr has talent. "The Dancing Faun" contains writing that is distinctively good. Doubtless it is only a prelude to something much stronger.'—*Academy.*

'As a work of art the book has the merit of brevity and smart writing; while the *dénoûement* is skilfully prepared, and comes as a surprise. If the book had been intended as a satire on the "new woman" sort of literature, it would have been most brilliant; but assuming it to be written in earnest, we can heartily praise the form of its construction without agreeing with the sentiments expressed.'—*St. James's Gazette.*

Shows considerable power and aptitude.'—*Saturday Review.*

'The book is extremely clever and some of the situations very striking, while there are sketches of character which really live. The final *dénoûement* might at first sight be thought impossible, but the effect on those who take part in it is so free of exaggeration, that we can almost imagine that such people are in our midst.'—*Guardian.*

POOR FOLK. Translated from the Russian of FEDOR
DOSTOIEVSKY. By LENA MILMAN. With an Intro-
duction by GEORGE MOORE, and a Title-page and Cover
Design by AUBREY BEARDSLEY. Crown 8vo, 3s. 6d. net.

'The book is cleverly translated. "Poor Folk" gains in reality and pathos
by the very means that in less skilful hands would be tedious and commonplace.'—*Spectator.*

'A charming story of the love of a Charles Lamb kind of old bachelor
for a young work-girl. Full of quiet humour and still more full of the
lachrymæ rerum.'—*Star.*

'Scenes of poignant realism, described with so admirable a blending of
humour and pathos that they haunt the memory.'—*Daily News.*

'No one will read it attentively without feeling both its power and its
pathos.'—*Scotsman.*

'The book is one of great pathos and absorbing interest. Miss Milman
has given us an admirable version of it which will commend itself to every
one who cares for good literature.'—*Glasgow Herald.*

'These things seem small, but in the hands of Dostoievsky they make
a work of genius.'—*Black and White.*

'One of the most pathetic things in all literature, heartrending just
because its tragedy is so repressed.'—*Bookman.*

'As to novels, the very finest I have read of late or for long is "Poor Folk,
by Fedor Dostoievsky, translated by Miss Lena Milman.'—*Truth.*

'A book to be read for the merits of its execution. The translator by
the way has turned it into excellent English.'—*Pall Mall Gazette.*

'The narrative vibrates with feeling, and these few unstudied letters convey to us a cry from the depths of a famished human soul. As far as we
can judge, the English rendering, though simple, retains that ring of
emotion which must distinguish the original.'—*Westminster Review.*

'One of the most striking studies in plain and simple realism which was
ever written.'—*Daily Telegraph.*

'"Poor Folk" is certainly a vivid and pathetic story.'—*Globe.*

'A triumph of realistic art—a masterpiece of a great writer.'—*Morning
Post.*

'Dostoievsky's novel has met with that rare advantage, a really good
translator.'—*Queen.*

'This admirable translation of a great author.'—*Liverpool Mercury.*

'"Poor Folk" Englished does not read like a translation—indubitably a
masterpiece.'—*Literary World.*

'Told with a gradually deepening intensity and force, a pathetic truth-
fulness which lives in the memory.'—*Leeds Mercury.*

'What Charles Dickens in his attempts to reproduce the sentiment and
pathos of the humble deceived himself and others into thinking that he did,
that Fedor Dostoievsky actually does.' —*Manchester Guardian.*

'It is a story that leaves the reader almost stunned. Miss Milman's
translation is admirable.'—*Gentlewoman.*

'The translation appears to be well done so far as we have compared it
with the original.'—W. R. MORFILL in *The Academy.*

'A most impressive and characteristic specimen of Russian fiction.
Those to whom Russian is a sealed book will be duly grateful to the translator (who has acquitted herself excellently), to Mr. Moore, and to the
publisher for this presentment of Dostoievsky's remarkable novel.'—*Times.*

A CHILD OF THE AGE.   By Francis Adams.   Title-page and Cover Design by Aubrey Beardsley.   Crown 8vo, 3s. 6d. net.

'English or foreign, there is no work among those now before me which is so original as that of the late Francis Adams.   "A Child of the Age" is original, moving, often fascinating.'—*Academy.*

'A great deal of cleverness and perhaps something more has gone to the writing of "A Child of the Age."'—*Vanity Fair.*

'It comes recognisably near to great excellence.   There is a love episode in this book which is certainly fine.   Clearly conceived and expressed with point.'—*Pall Mall Gazette.*

'Those whose actual experience or natural intuition will enable them to see beneath the mere narrative, will appreciate the perfect art with which a boy of nineteen—this was the author's age when the book was written—has treated one of the most delicate subjects on which a man can write—the history of his own innermost feelings.'—*Weekly Sun.*

'The book possesses a depth and clearness of insight, a delicacy of touch, and a brilliancy and beauty of style very remarkable in so young a writer.' —*Weekly Scotsman.*

'"A Child of the Age" is as fully saturated with the individuality of its author as "Wuthering Heights" was saturated with the individuality of Emily Brontë.'—*Daily Chronicle.*

'I am writing about the book because it is one you should read, for it is typical of a certain sort of character and contains some indubitable excellences.'—*Pall Mall Budget.*

'Not faultless, indeed, but touched with the magic of real poetry; without the elaborate carving of the chisel.   The love incident is exquisite and exquisitely told.   "Rosy" lives; her emotions stir us.   Wonderfully suggested in several parts of the work is the severe irony of nature before profound human suffering.'—*Saturday Review.*

'There is a bloom of romance upon their story which recalls Lucy and Richard Feverel. . . . . It is rarely that a novelist is able to suffuse his story with the first rosy purity of passion as Mr. Adams has done in this book.'—*Realm.*

'Only a man of big talent could have produced it.'—*Literary World.*

'A tale of fresh originality, deep spiritual meaning, and exceptional power.   It fairly buds, blossoms, and fruits with suggestions that search the human spirit through.   No similar production has come from the hand of any author in our time.   It exalts, inspires, comforts, and strengthens all together.   It instructs by suggestion, spiritualises the thought by its elevating and purifying narrative, and feeds the hungering spirit with food it is only too ready to accept and assimilate.'—*Boston Courier, U.S.A.*

'It is a remarkable work—as a pathological study almost unsurpassed. It produces the impression of a photograph from life, so vividly realistic is the treatment.   To this result the author's style, with its fidelity of microscopic detail, doubtless contributes.'—*Evening Traveller, U.S.A.*

'The story by Francis Adams is one to read slowly, and then to read a second time.   It is powerfully written, full of strong suggestion, unlike, in fact, anything we have recently read.   What he would have done in the way of literary creation, had he lived, is, of course, only a matter of conjecture.   What he did we have before us in this remarkable book.'—*Boston Advertiser, U.S.A.*

Second Edition now ready.

THE GREAT GOD PAN AND THE INMOST LIGHT.
By ARTHUR MACHEN.   With Title-page and Cover
Design by AUBREY BEARDSLEY.   Crown 8vo, 3s. 6d.
net.

'Since Mr. Stevenson played with the crucibles of science in "Dr.
Jekyll and Mr. Hyde" we have not encountered a more successful experiment of the sort.'—*Pall Mall Gazette.*

'Nothing so appalling as these tales has been given to publicity within
our remembrance; in which, nevertheless, such ghastly fictions as Poe's
"Telltale Heart," Bulwer's "The House and the Brain," and Le Fanu's
"In a Glass Darkly" still are vividly present. The supernatural element
is utilised with extraordinary power and effectiveness in both these blood-
chilling masterpieces.'—*Daily Telegraph.*

'He imparts the shudder of awe without giving rise to a feeling of disgust.
Let me strongly advise anyone anxious for a real, durable thrill, to get it.'—
Woman.

'A nightmarish business it is—suggested, seemingly, by "Dr. Jekyll and
Mr. Hyde"—and capital reading, we should say, for ghouls and vampires
in their leisure moments.'—*Daily Chronicle.*

'The rest we leave for those whose nerves are strong, merely saying that
since "Dr. Jekyll and Mr. Hyde," we have read nothing so uncanny.'—
The Literary World.

'The literature of the "supernatural" has recently been supplemented
by two striking books, which carry on with much ability the traditions of
Sheridan Le Fanu: one is "The Great God Pan," by Arthur Machen.'—
Star.

'Will arouse the sort of interest that was created by "Dr. Jekyll and
Mr. Hyde."   The tales present a frankly impossible horror, which, nevertheless, kindles the imagination and excites a powerful curiosity.   It is
almost a book of genius, and we are not sure that the safeguarding adverb
is not superfluous.'—*Birmingham Post.*

'The coarser terrors of Edgar Allen Poe do not leave behind them the
shudder that one feels at the shadowed devil-mysteries of "The Great God
Pan."'—*Liverpool Mercury.*

'If any one labours under a burning desire to experience the sensation
familiarly known as making one's flesh creep, he can hardly do better than
read "The Great God Pan."'—*Speaker.*

'For sheer gruesome horror Mr. Machen's story, "The Great God Pan,"
surpasses anything that has been published for a long time.'—*Scotsman.*

'Nothing more striking or more skilful than this book has been produced
in the way of what one may call Borderland fiction since Mr. Stevenson's
indefatigable Brownies gave the world "Dr. Jekyll and Mr. Hyde."'—
Glasgow Herald.

'The mysteries he deals with lie far beyond the reach of ordinary human
experience, and as they are vague, though so horror-producing, he wisely
treats them with a reticence that, while it accords with the theme, im-
mensely heightens the effect.'—*Dundee Advertiser.*

'The author is an artist, and tells his tale with reticence and grace,
hinting the demoniac secret at first obscurely, and only gradually permit-
ting the reader to divine how near to us are the infernal powers, and how
terribly they satiate their lusts and wreak their malice upon mankind. It
is a work of something like genius, fascinating and fearsome.'—*Bradford
Observer.*

'They are fitting companions to the famous stories by Edgar Allan Poe both in matter and style,'—*Boston Home Journal, U.S.A.*

'They are horror stories, the horror being of the vague psychologic kind and dependent in each case upon a man of science, who tries to effect a change in individual personality by an operation upon the brain cells. The implied lesson is that it is dangerous and unwise to seek to probe the mystery separating mind and matter. These sketches are extremely strong, and we guarantee the shivers to any one who reads them.'—*Hartford Courant, U.S.A.*

Fourth Edition now ready.

DISCORDS. By GEORGE EGERTON. With Title-page and Cover Design by AUBREY BEARDSLEY. Crown 8vo, 3s. 6d. net.

'We have the heights as well as the depths of life. The transforming touch of beauty is upon it, of that poetry of conception beneath whose spell nothing is ugly or unclean.'—*Star.*

'The writer is a warm-blooded enthusiast, not a cold-blooded "scientist." In the long run perhaps it will do some good.'—*National Observer.*

'The power and passion which every reader felt in "Keynotes" are equally present in this new volume. But there is also in at least equal measure that artistic force and skill which went so far to overcome the repugnance which many felt to the painful dissection of feminine nature.'—*North British Daily Mail.*

'Force of conception and power of vivid presentment mark these sketches, and are sure to impress all who read them.'—*Birmingham Post.*

'Written with all "George Egerton's" eloquence and fervour.'—*Yorkshire Herald.*

'It almost takes one's breath away by its prodigious wrong-headedness, its sheer impudence.'—MR. A. B. WALKLEY in *The Morning Leader.*

'The wonderful power of observation, the close analysis and the really brilliant writing revealed in parts of this volume . . . . "George Egerton" would seem to be well equipped for the task.'—*Cork Examiner.*

'Readers who have a leaning to psychological fiction, and who revel in such studies of character as George Meredith's "Diana of the Crossways" will find much to interest them in these clever stories.'—*Western Daily Press.*

'There is no escape from the fact that it is vividly interesting.'—*The Christian World.*

'With all her realism there is a refinement and a pathos and a brilliance of style that lift the book into a region altogether removed from the merely sensational or the merely repulsive. It is a book that one might read with a pencil in his hand, for it is studded with many fine, vivid passages.'—*Weekly Scotsman.*

'She has many fine qualities. Her work throbs with temperament, and here and there we come upon touches that linger in the memory as of things felt and seen, not read of.'—*Daily News.*

'Mrs. Grundy, to whom they would be salutary, will not be induced to read either "Keynotes" or "Discords."'—*Westminster Gazette.*

'What an absorbing, wonderful book it is : How absolutely sincere, and how finely wrong! George Egerton may be what the indefatigable Mr. Zangwill calls a one-I'd person, but she is a literary artist of exceptional endowment—probably a genius.'—*Woman.*

'She has given, times without number, examples of her ripening powers that astonish us. Her themes astound; her audacity is tremendous. In the many great passages an advance is proved that is little short of amazing.'—*Literary World*.

'Interesting and skilfully written.'—*Sunday Times*.

'A series of undoubtedly clever stories, told with a poetic dreaminess which softens the rugged truths of which they treat. Mothers might benefit themselves and convey help to young girls who are about to be married by the perusal of its pages.'—*Liverpool Mercury*.

'They are the work of an author of considerable power, not to say genius. —*Scotsman*.

'The book is true to human nature, for the author has genius, and, let us add, has heart. It is representative; it is, in the hackneyed phrase, a human document.'—*Speaker*.

'It is another note in the great chorus of revolt . . . on the whole clearer, more eloquent, and braver than almost any I have yet heard.'— T. P. ('Book of the Week'), *Weekly Sun*, December 30.

'These masterly word-sketches.'—*Daily Telegraph*.

'Were it possible to have my favourite sketches and stories from both volumes ("Keynotes" and "Discords") bound together in one, I should look upon myself as a very fortunate traveller; one who had great pleasure, if not exactly happiness, within her reach.'—*Lady's Pictorial*.

'But in all this there is a rugged grandeur of style, a keen analysis of motive, and a deepness of pathos that stamp George Egerton as one of the greatest women writers of the day.'—*Boston Traveller, U.S.A.*

'The story of the child, of the girl, and of the woman is told, and told by one to whom the mysteries of the life of each are familiarly known, In their very truth, as the writer has so subtly analysed her triple characters, they sadden one to think that such things must be; yet as they are real, they are bound to be disclosed by somebody, and in due time.'—*Boston Courier, U.S.A.*

Ninth Edition just ready.

THE WOMAN WHO DID. By Grant Allen. With Title-page and Cover Design by Aubrey Beardsley. Crown 8vo, 3s. 6d. net.

'There is not a sensual thought or suggestion throughout the whole volume. Though I dislike and disbelieve in his gospel, I thoroughly respect Mr. Grant Allen for having stated it so honourably and so bravely.' —*Academy*.

'Even its bitterest enemies must surely feel some thrill of admiration for its courage. It is, once more, one philosopher against the world. Not in our day, perhaps, can it be decided which is right, Mr. Grant Allen, or the world. Perhaps our children's children will some day be canonising Mr. Grant Allen for the very book for which to-day he stands a much greater chance of being stoned, and happy lovers of the new era bless the name of the man who, almost single-handed, fought the battle of Free Love. Time alone can say. . . . None but the most foolish or malignant reader of 'The Woman Who Did' can fail to recognise the noble purpose which animates its pages. . . . Label it as one will, it remains a clever, stimulating book. A real enthusiasm for humanity blazes through every page of this, in many ways, remarkable and significant little book.'—*Sketch*.

'The book is interesting, as embodying the carefully thought-out theories of so distinguished a writer.'—*Literary World*.

'Mr. Grant Allen has undoubtedly produced an epoch-making book, and one which will be a living voice when most of the novels of this generation have passed away into silence. It is epoch-making in the sense that "Uncle Tom's Cabin" was;—the literary merits of that work were by no means great, but yet it rang like a tocsin through the land, arousing mankind to a sense of the slavery under which a large portion of humanity suffered.'—*Humanitarian.*

'Interesting, and even absorbing.'—*Weekly Sun.*

'His sincerity is undeniable. And in the mouth of Herminia are some very noble and eloquent passages upon the wrongs of our marriage system.'—*Pall Mall Gazette.*

'A tale of purity and innocence unparalleled since the "Garden of Eden" or "Paul and Virginia."'—*Daily Express.*

'A remarkable and powerful story. It increases our respect for Mr. Allen's ability, nor do we feel inclined to join in throwing stones at him as a perverter of our morals and our social institutions. However widely we may differ from Mr. Allen's views on many important questions, we are bound to recognise his sincerity, and to respect him accordingly.'—*Speaker.*

'The story is as remarkable for its art as its daring, and well deserves a place in the remarkable series in which it has been published.'—*The Scotsman.*

'Herminia is a rare and fine creature.'—*Daily Chronicle.*

'An artist in words and a writer of deep feeling has lavished his best powers in the production of "The Woman Who Did." The story is charmingly told. Delineated with a delicacy and strength of touch that cannot but delight the most fastidious reader. Mr. Grant Allen draws a picture of a sweet and pure and beautiful woman. The book is very beautiful and very sad.'—*Liverpool Mercury.*

'The book (for it is well written and clever) ought to be the last note in the chorus of revolt. For it proves to demonstration the futility of the attempt.'—*Sun.*

'We cannot too highly commend the conspicuous and transparent purity of the handling.'—*Public Opinion.*

'He conclusively shows that if the marriage laws need revision, yet the sweetness and seemliness of home, the dignity of woman as mother or as man's helpmeet, are rooted in the sanctity of wedlock.'—*Daily News.*

'Mr. Grant Allen deserves thanks for treating with such delicacy a problem which stands in such pressing need of solution as the reform of our stern marriage laws.'—*Echo.*

'Its merits are large and its interest profound.'—*Weekly Scotsman.*

'It may not merit praise, but it merits reading.'—*Saturday Review.*

Just published.

PRINCE ZALESKI. By M. P. SHIEL. With Title-page by AUBREY BEARDSLEY. Crown 8vo, 3s. 6d. net.

'Mr. M. P. Shiel has in this volume produced something which is always rare, and which is every year becoming a greater rarity—a work of literary invention characterised by substantial novelty. We have Poe's analysis and Poe's glamour, but they are no longer distinct; they are combined in a new synthesis which stamps a new imaginative impression. A finely wrought structure in which no single line impairs the symmetry and proportion. One of the most boldly-planned and strikingly-executed stories of its kind which has appeared for many a long day. We believe there is nothing in " Prince Zaleski" which that great inventor and masterly manipulator of the spoils of invention (Poe) would have disdained to father.'—*Daily Chronicle*.

'Should obtain popularity. Written in an easy and clear style. The author shows an amount of ingenuity and capacity for plot considerably above the average. The reader will find it difficult to put the book down before he has satisfied his curiosity to the last page.'—*Weekly Sun*.

'The Prince was a Sherlock Holmes, with this difference : that while yielding nothing to Conan Doyle's hero in mere intellectual agility, he had that imaginative insight which makes poets more frequently than detectives. Sherlock Holmes was a clever but essentially commonplace man. Prince Zaleski was a great man, simply. Enthralling . . . once begun they insist on being finished. Broadly and philosophically conceived, and put together with rare narrative skill, and feeling for effect.' —*Woman*.

'There is a strange, fantastic ingenuity in all the stories, while a strong dash of mysticism gives them a peculiar flavour that differentiates them from the ordinary detective story. They are clever and curious, and will appeal to all lovers of the transcendental and improbable.'—*The Scotsman*.

'Thoroughly entertaining, and the chief figure is undeniably picturesque.'—*Yorkshire Post*.

'An abundance of ingenuity and quaint out-of-the-way learning mark the three stories contained in this volume.'—*Liverpool Mercury*.

'He has imparted to the three tales in this volume something of that atmosphere of eerie fantasy which Poe knew how to conjure, proceeding by the analysis of a baffling intricacy of detail to an unforeseen conclusion. The themes and their treatment are alike highly imaginative.'—*Daily News*.

'Manifestly written by one of Poe's true disciples. His analytical skill is not that of the detective, even of so brilliant a detective as Mr. Sherlock Holmes. Probably his exploits will interest the public far less than did those of Mr. Doyle's famous character ; but the select few, who can appreciate delicate work, will delight in them exceedingly.'—*Speaker*.

'Truth to tell we like our Sherlock better in his new dress. The book will please those who love a good old-fashioned riddle, and a good new-fangled answer.'—*National Observer*.

'Has genuine literary merit, and possesses entrancing interest. A kind of Sherlock Holmes, though of a far more finished type than Mr. Conan Doyle's famous creation. The remarkable ingenuity of Mr. Shiel—worthy of Edgar Allen Poe at his best—in tracing out the mystery surrounding the death of Lord Pharanx, the Stone of the Edmundsbury Monks, and the Suicide Society, constitutes a veritable *tour de force*. We have nothing but praise for this extraordinarily clever and interesting volume.'—*Whitehall Review*.

'Worked out very ingeniously, and we are thoroughly impressed by the Prince's mental powers.'—*Sunday Times*.

'A clever, extravagant, and lurid little book.'—*Westminster Gazette*.

List of Books

in

Belles Lettres

ALL BOOKS IN THIS CATALOGUE
ARE PUBLISHED AT NET PRICES

1895

Telegraphic Address—
'BODLEIAN, LONDON'

List of Books

IN

BELLES LETTRES

(*Including some Transfers*)

Published by John Lane

𝕿𝖍𝖊 𝕭𝖔𝖉𝖑𝖊𝖞 𝕳𝖊𝖆𝖉

VIGO STREET, LONDON, W.

N.B.—The Authors and Publisher reserve the right of reprinting any book in this list if a new edition is called for, except in cases where a stipulation has been made to the contrary, and of printing a separate edition of any of the books for America irrespective of the numbers to which the English editions are limited. The numbers mentioned do not include copies sent to the public libraries, nor those sent for review.

Most of the books are published simultaneously in England and America, and in many instances the names of the American Publishers are appended.

━━━━━━◆━━━━━━

ADAMS (FRANCIS).

    ESSAYS IN MODERNITY. Crown 8vo. 5s. net. [*Shortly.*
      Chicago: Stone & Kimball.

    A CHILD OF THE AGE. (*See* KEYNOTES SERIES.)

ALLEN (GRANT).

    THE LOWER SLOPES: A Volume of Verse. With Title-page and Cover Design by J. ILLINGWORTH KAY. 600 copies. Crown 8vo. 5s. net.
      Chicago: Stone & Kimball.

    THE WOMAN WHO DID. (*See* KEYNOTES SERIES.)

BEARDSLEY (AUBREY).

THE STORY OF VENUS AND TANNHÄUSER, in which is set forth an exact account of the Manner of State held by Madam Venus, Goddess and Meretrix, under the famous Hörselberg, and containing the adventures of Tannhäuser in that place, his repentance, his journeying to Rome, and return to the loving mountain. By AUBREY BEARDSLEY. With 20 full-page illustrations, numerous ornaments, and a cover from the same hand. Sq. 16mo. 10s. 6d. net. [*In preparation.*

BEDDOES (T. L.).

See GOSSE (EDMUND).

BEECHING (REV. H. C.).

IN A GARDEN: Poems. With Title-page designed by ROGER FRY. Crown 8vo. 5s. net.
New York: Macmillan & Co.

BENSON (ARTHUR CHRISTOPHER).

LYRICS. Fcap. 8vo., buckram. 5s. net.
New York: Macmillan & Co.

BROTHERTON (MARY).

ROSEMARY FOR REMEMBRANCE. With Title-page and Cover Design by WALTER WEST. Fcap. 8vo. 3s. 6d. net.

CAMPBELL (GERALD).

THE JONESES AND THE ASTERISKS. With 6 Illustrations and a Title-page by F. H. TOWNSEND. Fcap. 8vo. 3s. 6d. net. [*In preparation.*

CASTLE (MRS. EGERTON).

MY LITTLE LADY ANNE: A Romance. Sq. 16mo. 2s. 6d. net. [*In preparation.*

CASTLE (EGERTON).

See STEVENSON (ROBERT LOUIS).

CROSS (VICTORIA).

CONSUMMATION: A Novel. Crown 8vo. 4s. 6d. net. [*In preparation.*

DALMON (C. W.).

SONG FAVOURS. With a specially-designed Title-page. Sq. 16mo. 4s. 6d. net. [*In preparation.*

D'ARCY (ELLA).

MONOCHROMES. (*See* KEYNOTES SERIES.)

DAVIDSON (JOHN).

PLAYS: An Unhistorical Pastoral; A Romantic Farce; Bruce, a Chronicle Play; Smith, a Tragic Farce; Scaramouch in Naxos, a Pantomime, with a Frontispiece and Cover Design by AUBREY BEARDSLEY. Printed at the Ballantyne Press. 500 copies. Small 4to. 7s. 6d. net.
> Chicago: Stone & Kimball.

FLEET STREET ECLOGUES. Fcap. 8vo, buckram. 5s. net.   [*Out of Print at present.*

A RANDOM ITINERARY AND A BALLAD. With a Frontispiece and Title-page by LAURENCE HOUSMAN. 600 copies. Fcap. 8vo, Irish Linen. 5s. net.
> Boston: Copeland & Day.

BALLADS AND SONGS. With a Title-page and Cover Design by WALTER WEST. Third Edition. Fcap. 8vo, buckram. 5s. net.
> Boston: Copeland & Day.

DAWE (W. CARLTON).

YELLOW AND WHITE. (*See* KEYNOTES SERIES.)

DE TABLEY (LORD).

POEMS, DRAMATIC AND LYRICAL. By JOHN LEICESTER WARREN (Lord De Tabley). Illustrations and Cover Design by C. S. RICKETTS. Second Edition. Crown 8vo. 7s. 6d. net.
> New York: Macmillan & Co.

POEMS, DRAMATIC AND LYRICAL. Second Series, uniform in binding with the former volume. Crown 8vo. 5s. net.
> New York: Macmillan & Co.

DIX (GERTRUDE).

THE GIRL FROM THE FARM. (*See* KEYNOTES SERIES.)

DOSTOIEVSKY (F.).

See KEYNOTES SERIES, Vol. III.

ECHEGARAY (JOSÉ).
>   *See* LYNCH (HANNAH).

EGERTON (GEORGE).
>   KEYNOTES. (*See* KEYNOTES SERIES.)
>   DISCORDS. (*See* KEYNOTES SERIES.)
>   YOUNG OFEG'S DITTIES. A translation from the Swedish
>   of OLA HANSSON. Crown 8vo. 3s. 6d. net.
>>   Boston : Roberts Bros.

FARR (FLORENCE).
>   THE DANCING FAUN. (*See* KEYNOTES SERIES.)

FLETCHER (J. S.).
>   THE WONDERFUL WAPENTAKE. By 'A SON OF THE
>   SOIL.' With 18 full-page Illustrations by J. A.
>   SYMINGTON. Crown 8vo. 5s. 6d. net.
>>   Chicago : A. C. M'Clurg & Co.

GALE (NORMAN).
>   ORCHARD SONGS. With Title-page and Cover Design
>   by J. ILLINGWORTH KAY. Fcap. 8vo, Irish Linen.
>   5s. net.
>   Also a Special Edition limited in number on hand-made paper
>   bound in English vellum. £1, 1s. net.
>>   New York : G. P. Putnam's Sons.

GARNETT (RICHARD).
>   POEMS. With Title-page by J. ILLINGWORTH KAY.
>   350 copies. Crown 8vo. 5s. net.
>>   Boston : Copeland & Day.
>   DANTE, PETRARCH, CAMOENS, cxxiv Sonnets, rendere
>   in English. Crown 8vo. 5s. net. [*In preparation.*

GEARY (NEVILL).
>   A LAWYER'S WIFE : A Novel. Crown 8vo. 4s. 6d.
>   net. [*In preparation.*

GOSSE (EDMUND).
>   THE LETTERS OF THOMAS LOVELL BEDDOES. Now
>   first edited. Pott 8vo. 5s. net.
>   Also 25 copies large paper. 12s. 6d. net.
>>   New York : Macmillan & Co.

GRAHAME (KENNETH).

PAGAN PAPERS : A Volume of Essays.   With Title-page by AUBREY BEARDSLEY.   Fcap. 8vo.   5s. net.
Chicago : Stone & Kimball.

THE GOLDEN AGE.   Crown 8vo.   3s. 6d. net.
Chicago : Stone & Kimball.   [*In preparation.*

GREENE (G. A.).

ITALIAN LYRISTS OF TO-DAY.   Translations in the original metres from about thirty-five living Italian poets, with bibliographical and biographical notes. Crown 8vo.   5s. net.
New York : Macmillan & Co.

GREENWOOD (FREDERICK).

IMAGINATION IN DREAMS.   Crown 8vo.   5s. net.
New York : Macmillan & Co.

HAKE (T. GORDON).

A SELECTION FROM HIS POEMS.   Edited by Mrs. MEYNELL.   With a Portrait after D. G. ROSSETTI, and a Cover Design by GLEESON WHITE.   Crown 8vo.   5s. net.
Chicago : Stone & Kimball.

HANSSON (LAURA MARHOLM).

MODERN WOMEN : Six Psychological Sketches.   [Sophia Kovalevsky, George Egerton, Eleanora Duse, Amalie Skram, Marie Bashkirtseff, A. Edgren Leffler].   Translated from the German by HERMIONE RAMSDEN. Crown 8vo.   3s. 6d. net.   [*In preparation.*

HANSSON (OLA).   *See* EGERTON.

HARLAND (HENRY).

GREY ROSES.   (*See* KEYNOTES SERIES.)

HAYES (ALFRED).

THE VALE OF ARDEN AND OTHER POEMS.   With a Title-page and a Cover designed by E. H. NEW.
Fcap. 8vo.   3s. 6d. net.
Also 25 copies large paper.   15s. net.

HEINEMANN (WILLIAM)

THE FIRST STEP   A Dramatic Moment.   Small 4to. 3s. 6d. net.

HOPPER (NORA).

BALLADS IN PROSE. With a Title-page and Cover by WALTER WEST. Sq. 16mo. 5s. net.

Boston: Roberts Bros.

HOUSMAN (LAURENCE).

GREEN ARRAS: Poems. With Illustrations by the Author. Crown 8vo. 5s. net. [*In preparation.*

IRVING (LAURENCE).

GODEFROI AND YOLANDE: A Play. With three Illustrations by AUBREY BEARDSLEY. Sm. 4to. 5s. net. [*In preparation.*

JAMES (W. P.).

ROMANTIC PROFESSIONS: A Volume of Essays. With Title-page designed by J. ILLINGWORTH KAY. Crown 8vo. 5s. net.

New York: Macmillan & Co.

JOHNSON (LIONEL).

THE ART OF THOMAS HARDY: Six Essays. With Etched Portrait by WM. STRANG, and Bibliography by JOHN LANE. Second Edition. Crown 8vo. 5s. 6d. net.

Also 150 copies, large paper, with proofs of the portrait. £1, 1s. net.

New York: Dodd, Mead & Co.

JOHNSON (PAULINE).

WHITE WAMPUM: Poems. With a Title-page and Cover Design by E. H. NEW. Crown 8vo. 5s. net. [*In preparation.*

JOHNSTONE (C. E.).

BALLADS OF BOY AND BEAK. Sq. 32mo. 2s. 6d. net. [*In preparation.*

KEYNOTES SERIES.

Each volume with specially designed Title-page by AUBREY BEARDSLEY. Crown 8vo, cloth. 3s. 6d. net.

Vol. I. KEYNOTES. By GEORGE EGERTON. [*Sixth edition now ready.*

Vol. II. THE DANCING FAUN. By FLORENCE FARR.

Vol. III. POOR FOLK. Translated from the Russian of F. Dostoievsky by LENA MILMAN. With a Preface by GEORGE MOORE.

Vol. IV. A CHILD OF THE AGE. By FRANCIS ADAMS.

KEYNOTES SERIES—*continued.*

Vol.   V. THE GREAT GOD PAN AND THE INMOST
        LIGHT. By ARTHUR MACHEN.
                    [*Second edition now ready.*

Vol.   VI. DISCORDS. By GEORGE EGERTON.
                    [*Fourth edition now ready.*

Vol.   VII. PRINCE ZALESKI. By M. P. SHIEL.

Vol.   VIII. THE WOMAN WHO DID. By GRANT ALLEN.
                    [*Eleventh edition now ready.*

Vol.   IX. WOMEN'S TRAGEDIES. By H. D. LOWRY.

Vol.   X. GREY ROSES. By HENRY HARLAND.

Vol.   XI. AT THE FIRST CORNER AND OTHER STORIES.
        By H. B. MARRIOTT WATSON.

The following Volumes are in rapid preparation.

Vol.   XII. MONOCHROMES. By ELLA D'ARCY.

Vol.   XIII. AT THE RELTON ARMS. By EVELYN SHARP.

Vol.   XIV. THE GIRL FROM THE FARM. By GERTRUDE
        DIX.

Vol.   XV. THE MIRROR OF MUSIC. By STANLEY V.
        MAKOWER.

Vol.   XVI. YELLOW AND WHITE. By W. CARLTON
        DAWE.

Vol.   XVII. THE MOUNTAIN LOVERS. By FIONA
        MACLEOD.

Vol.   XVIII. THE THREE IMPOSTORS. By ARTHUR
        MACHEN.
        Boston: Roberts Bros.

LANDER (HARRY).

WEIGHED IN THE BALANCE: A Novel. Crown 8vo.
    4s. 6d. net.   [*In preparation.*

LANG (ANDREW).
    See STODDART.

LEATHER (R. K.).

VERSES. 250 copies. Fcap. 8vo. 3s. net.
    Transferred by the Author to the present Publisher.

LE GALLIENNE (RICHARD).

PROSE FANCIES. With Portrait of the Author by
    WILSON STEER. Fourth Edition. Crown 8vo. Purple
    cloth. 5s. net.
    Also a limited large paper edition. 12s. 6d. net.
    New York: G. P. Putnam's Sons.

LE GALLIENNE (RICHARD).

> THE BOOK BILLS OF NARCISSUS, An Account rendered by RICHARD LE GALLIENNE. Third Edition. With a Frontispiece. Crown 8vo. Purple cloth. 3s. 6d. net.
> Also 50 copies on large paper. 8vo. 10s. 6d. net.
> New York: G. P. Putnam's Sons.

> ROBERT LOUIS STEVENSON, AN ELEGY, AND OTHER POEMS, MAINLY PERSONAL. With Etched Title-page by D. Y. CAMERON. Cr. 8vo. Purple cloth. 4s. 6d. net.
> Also 75 copies on large paper. 8vo. 12s. 6d. net. [In preparation.
> Boston: Copeland & Day.

> ENGLISH POEMS. Fourth Edition, revised. Crown 8vo. Purple cloth. 4s. 6d. net. [In preparation.
> Boston: Copeland & Day.

> RETROSPECTIVE REVIEWS, A LITERARY LOG, 1891-1895. Crown 8vo. Purple cloth. 5s. net.
> [In preparation.

> GEORGE MEREDITH: Some Characteristics. With a Bibliography (much enlarged) by JOHN LANE, portrait, etc. Fourth Edition. Cr. 8vo. Purple cloth. 5s. 6d. net.

> THE RELIGION OF A LITERARY MAN. 5th thousand. Crown 8vo. Purple cloth. 3s. 6d. net.
> Also a special rubricated edition on hand-made paper. 8vo. 10s. 6d. net.
> New York: G. P. Putnam's Sons.

LOWRY (H. D.).

> WOMEN'S TRAGEDIES. (See KEYNOTES SERIES.)

LUCAS (WINIFRED).

> A VOLUME OF POEMS. Fcap. 8vo. 4s. 6d. net.
> [In preparation.

LYNCH (HANNAH).

> THE GREAT GALEOTO AND FOLLY OR SAINTLINESS. Two Plays, from the Spanish of JOSÉ ECHEGARAY, with an Introduction. Small 4to. 5s. 6d. net.
> [In preparation.

MACHEN (ARTHUR).

> THE GREAT GOD PAN. (See KEYNOTES SERIES.)
> THE THREE IMPOSTORS. (See KEYNOTES SERIES.)

MACLEOD (FIONA).

> THE MOUNTAIN LOVERS. (See KEYNOTES SERIES.)

MAKOWER (STANLEY V.).
THE MIRROR OF MUSIC. (*See* KEYNOTES SERIES.)

MARZIALS (THEO.).
THE GALLERY OF PIGEONS AND OTHER POEMS.   Post
8vo.   4s. 6d. net.   [*Very few remain.*
Transferred by the Author to the present Publisher.

MATHEW (FRANK).
THE WOOD OF THE BRAMBLES : A Novel.   Crown 8vo.
4s. 6d. net.   [*In preparation.*

MEREDITH (GEORGE)
THE FIRST PUBLISHED PORTRAIT OF THIS AUTHOR,
engraved on the wood by W. BISCOMBE GARDNER,
after the painting by G. F. WATTS.   Proof copies on
Japanese vellum, signed by painter and engraver.
£1, 1s. net.

MEYNELL (MRS.), (ALICE C. THOMPSON).
POEMS. Fcap. 8vo.   3s. 6d. net. [*Out of Print at present.*
A few of the 50 large paper copies (First Edition) remain, 12s. 6d. net.
THE RHYTHM OF LIFE AND OTHER ESSAYS.   Second
Edition.   Fcap. 8vo.   3s. 6d. net.
A few of the 50 large paper copies (First Edition) remain.   12s. 6d. net.
See also HAKE.

MILLER (JOAQUIN).
THE BUILDING OF THE CITY BEAUTIFUL.   Fcap. 8vo.
With a Decorated Cover.   5s. net.
Chicago : Stone & Kimball.

MILMAN (LENA).
DOSTOIEVSKY'S POOR FOLK.   (*See* KEYNOTES SERIES.)

MONKHOUSE (ALLAN).
BOOKS AND PLAYS : A Volume of Essays on Meredith,
Borrow, Ibsen, and others.   400 copies.   Crown 8vo.
5s. net.
Philadelphia : J. B. Lippincott Co.

MOORE (GEORGE).
See KEYNOTES SERIES, Vol. III.

NESBIT (E.).
A POMANDER OF VERSE.   With a Title-page and Cover
designed by LAURENCE HOUSMAN.   Crown 8vo.
5s. net.   [*In preparation.*

NETTLESHIP (J. T.).
ROBERT BROWNING : Essays and Thoughts. Third
Edition. With a Portrait. Crown 8vo. 5s. 6d. net.
New York : Chas. Scribner's Sons.

NOBLE (JAS. ASHCROFT).
THE SONNET IN ENGLAND AND OTHER ESSAYS. Title-
page and Cover Design by AUSTIN YOUNG. 600
copies. Crown 8vo. 5s. net.
Also 50 copies large paper. 12s. 6d. net.

O'SHAUGHNESSY (ARTHUR).
HIS LIFE AND HIS WORK. With Selections from his
Poems. By LOUISE CHANDLER MOULTON. Por-
trait and Cover Design. Fcap. 8vo. 5s. net.
Chicago : Stone & Kimball.

OXFORD CHARACTERS.
A series of lithographed portraits by WILL ROTHENSTEIN,
with text by F. YORK POWELL and others. To be
issued monthly in term. Each number will contain
two portraits. Parts I. to VI. ready. 200 sets only,
folio, wrapper, 5s. net per part; 25 special large
paper sets containing proof impressions of the portraits signed by the artist, 10s. 6d. net per part.

PETERS (WM. THEODORE).
POSIES OUT OF RINGS. Sq. 16mo. 3s. 6d. net.
[*In preparation.*

PISSARRO (LUCIEN).
THE QUEEN OF THE FISHES. A Story of the Valois,
adapted by MARGARET RUST, being a printed manu-
script, decorated with pictures and other ornaments,
cut on the wood by LUCIEN PISSARRO, and printed
by him in divers colours and in gold at his press
in Epping. Edition limited to 70 copies, each num-
bered and signed. Crown 8vo. on Japanese hand-
made paper, bound in vellum, £1 net.

PLARR (VICTOR).
IN THE DORIAN MOOD : Poems. Crown 8vo. 5s. net.
[*In preparation.*

RADFORD (DOLLIE).
SONGS AND OTHER VERSES. Fcap. 8vo. 4s. 6d. net.
[*In preparation.*

RAMSDEN (HERMIONE).
See HANSSON.

RICKETTS (C. S.) AND C. H. SHANNON.
HERO AND LEANDER. By CHRISTOPHER MARLOWE and GEORGE CHAPMAN. With Borders, Initials, and Illustrations designed and engraved on the wood by C. S. RICKETTS and C. H. SHANNON. Bound in English vellum and gold. 200 copies only. 35s. net.
Boston : Copeland & Day.

RHYS (ERNEST).
A LONDON ROSE AND OTHER RHYMES. With Title-page designed by SELWYN IMAGE. 350 copies. Crown 8vo. 5s. net.
New York : Dodd, Mead & Co.

ROBINSON (C. NEWTON).
THE VIOL OF LOVE. With Ornaments and Cover design by LAURENCE HOUSMAN. Crown 8vo.   net.
[*In preparation.*

ST. CYRES (LORD).
THE LITTLE FLOWERS OF ST. FRANCIS: A new rendering into English of the Fioretti di San Francesco. Crown 8vo. 5s. net.   [*In preparation.*

SHARP (EVELYN).
AT THE RELTON ARMS. (*See* KEYNOTES SERIES.)

SHIEL (M. P.).
PRINCE ZALESKI. (*See* KEYNOTES SERIES.)

STACPOOLE (H. DE VERE).
DEATH, THE KNIGHT AND THE LADY. Sq. 16mo. 2s. 6d. net.   [*In preparation.*

STEVENSON (ROBERT LOUIS).
PRINCE OTTO. A Rendering in French by EGERTON CASTLE. Crown 8vo. 5s. net.   [*In preparation.*
Also 100 copies on large paper, uniform in size with the Edinburgh Edition of the Works.

STODDART (THOS. TOD).
THE DEATH WAKE. With an Introduction by ANDREW LANG. Fcap. 8vo.   net.   [*In preparation.*

STREET (G. S.).

    THE AUTOBIOGRAPHY OF A BOY. Passages selected by his friend G. S. S. With Title-page designed by C. W. FURSE. Fcap. 8vo. 3s. 6d. net.

        [Fourth Edition now ready.

    Philadelphia : J. B. Lippincott Co.

    MINIATURES AND MOODS. Fcap. 8vo. 3s. net.

    Transferred by the Author to the present Publisher.

SWETTENHAM (F. W.).

    MALAY SKETCHES. Crown 8vo. 5s. 6d. net.

        [In preparation.

TABB (JOHN B.).

    POEMS. Sq. 32mo. 4s. 6d. net.

    Boston : Copeland & Day.

TENNYSON (FREDERICK).

    POEMS OF THE DAY AND YEAR. Crown 8vo. 5s. net.

        [In preparation.

THIMM (C. A.).

    A COMPLETE BIBLIOGRAPHY OF THE ART OF FENCE, DUELLING, ETC. With Illustrations.

        [In preparation.

THOMPSON (FRANCIS).

    POEMS. With Frontispiece, Title-page, and Cover Design by LAURENCE HOUSMAN. Fourth Edition. Pott 4to. 5s. net.

    Boston : Copeland & Day.

    SONGS WING-TO-WING : An Offering to Two Sisters. Pott 4to. 5s. net. *[In preparation.*

TYNAN HINKSON (KATHARINE).

    CUCKOO SONGS. With Title-page and Cover Design by LAURENCE HOUSMAN. Fcap. 8vo. 5s. net.

    Boston : Copeland & Day.

    MIRACLE PLAYS. *[In preparation.*

WATSON (ROSAMUND MARRIOTT).

    VESPERTILIA AND OTHER POEMS. With a Title-page designed by R. ANNING BELL. Fcap. 8vo. 4s. 6d. net. *[In preparation.*

WATSON (H. B. MARRIOTT).

    AT THE FIRST CORNER. (*See* KEYNOTES SERIES.)

WATSON (WILLIAM).
    ODES AND OTHER POEMS. Fourth Edition. Fcap. 8vo, buckram. 4s. 6d. net.
      New York: Macmillan & Co.
    THE ELOPING ANGELS: A Caprice. Second Edition. Square 16mo, buckram. 3s. 6d. net.
      New York: Macmillan & Co.
    EXCURSIONS IN CRITICISM: being some Prose Recreations of a Rhymer. Second Edition. Cr. 8vo. 5s. net.
      New York: Macmillan & Co.
    THE PRINCE'S QUEST AND OTHER POEMS. With a Bibliographical Note added. Second Edition. Fcap. 8vo. 4s. 6d. net.

WATT (FRANCIS).
    THE LAW'S LUMBER ROOM. Fcap. 8vo. 3s. 6d. net.
                                  [*In preparation.*

WATTS (THEODORE).
    POEMS. Crown 8vo. 5s. net.   [*In preparation.*
    There will also be an Edition de Luxe *of this volume printed at the Kelmscott Press.*

WELLS (H. G.).
    SELECT CONVERSATIONS WITH AN UNCLE, SINCE DECEASED. With a Title-page designed by F. H. TOWNSEND. Fcap. 8vo. 3s. 6d. net. [*In preparation.*

WHARTON (H. T.).
    SAPPHO. Memoir, Text, Selected Renderings, and a Literal Translation by HENRY THORNTON WHARTON. With three Illustrations in photogravure, and a Cover designed by AUBREY BEARDSLEY. Fcap. 8vo. 7s. 6d. net.   [*In preparation.*

THE YELLOW BOOK
An Illustrated Quarterly

Vol. I. Fourth Edition, 272 pages, 15 Illustrations, Title-page, and a Cover Design. Cloth. Price 5s. net. Pott 4to.

The Literary Contributions by MAX BEERBOHM, A. C. BENSON, HUBERT CRACKANTHORPE, ELLA D'ARCY, JOHN DAVIDSON, GEORGE EGERTON, RICHARD GARNETT, EDMUND GOSSE, HENRY HARLAND, JOHN OLIVER HOBBES, HENRY JAMES, RICHARD LE GALLIENNE, GEORGE MOORE, GEORGE SAINTSBURY, FRED. M. SIMPSON, ARTHUR SYMONS, WILLIAM WATSON, ARTHUR WAUGH.

The Art Contributions by Sir FREDERIC LEIGHTON, P.R.A., AUBREY BEARDSLEY, R. ANNING BELL, CHARLES W. FURSE, LAURENCE HOUSMAN, J. T. NETTLESHIP, JOSEPH PENNELL, WILL ROTHENSTEIN, WALTER SICKERT.

Vol. II. Third Edition. Pott 4to, 364 pages, 23 Illustrations, and a New Title-page and Cover Design. Cloth. Price 5s. net.

The Literary Contributions by FREDERICK GREENWOOD, ELLA D'ARCY, CHARLES WILLEBY, JOHN DAVIDSON, HENRY HARLAND, DOLLIE RADFORD, CHARLOTTE M. MEW, AUSTIN DOBSON, V., O., C. S., KATHARINE DE MATTOS, PHILIP GILBERT HAMERTON, RONALD CAMP-BELL MACFIE, DAUPHIN MEUNIER, KENNETH GRAHAME, NORMAN GALE, NETTA SYRETT, HUBERT CRACKAN-THORPE, ALFRED HAYES, MAX BEERBOHM, WILLIAM WATSON, and HENRY JAMES.

The Art Contributions by WALTER CRANE, A. S. HARTRICK, AUBREY BEARDSLEY, ALFRED THORNTON, P. WILSON STEER, JOHN S. SARGENT, A.R.A., SYDNEY ADAMSON, WALTER SICKERT, W. BROWN MACDOUGAL, E. J. SULLIVAN, FRANCIS FORSTER, BERNHARD SICKERT, and AYMER VALLANCE.

A Special Feature of Volume II. is a frank criticism of the Literature and Art of Volume I. by PHILIP GILBERT HAMERTON.

Vol. III. Third Edition. Now Ready. Pott 4to, 280 pages, 15 Illustrations, and a New Title-page and Cover Design. Cloth. Price 5s. net.

The Literary Contributions by WILLIAM WATSON, KENNETH GRAHAME, ARTHUR SYMONS, ELLA D'ARCY, JOSÉ MARIA DE HÉRÉDIA, ELLEN M. CLERKE, HENRY HARLAND, THEO MARZIALS, ERNEST DOWSON, THEODORE WRATIS-LAW, ARTHUR MOORE, OLIVE CUSTANCE, LIONEL JOHN-SON, ANNIE MACDONELL, C. S., NORA HOPPER, S. CORNISH WATKINS, HUBERT CRACKANTHORPE, MORTON FULLERTON, LEILA MACDONALD, C. W. DALMON, MAX BEERBOHM, and JOHN DAVIDSON.

The Art Contributions by PHILIP BROUGHTON, GEORGE THOMSON, AUBREY BEARDSLEY, ALBERT FOSCHTER, WALTER SICKERT, P. WILSON STEER, WILLIAM HYDE, and MAX BEERBOHM.

Vol. IV.   Second Edition.   Now Ready.   Pott 4to, 285 pages,
16 Full-page Illustrations.   With New Title-page and
Cover Designs and a Double-page Supplement by Aubrey
Beardsley.   Price 5s. net.

The Literary Contributions by RICHARD LE GALLIENNE,
HENRY HARLAND, GRAHAM R. TOMSON, H. B. MARRIOTT
WATSON, DOLF WYLLARDE, MÉNIE MURIEL DOWIE,
OLIVE CUSTANCE, JAMES ASHCROFT NOBLE, LEILA MAC-
DONALD, C. S., RICHARD GARNETT, VICTORIA CROSS,
CHARLES SYDNEY, KENNETH GRAHAME, C. NEWTON
ROBINSON, NORMAN HAPGOOD, E. NESBIT, MARION HEP-
WORTH DIXON, C. W. DALMON, EVELYN SHARP, MAX
BEERBOHM, and JOHN DAVIDSON.

The Art Contributions by H. J. DRAPER, WILLIAM HYDE,
WALTER SICKERT, PATTEN WILSON, W. W. RUSSELL,
A. S. HARTRICK, CHARLES CONDER, WILL ROTHENSTEIN,
MISS SUMNER, P. WILSON STEER, and AUBREY BEARDS-
LEY.

Vol. V.   Now Ready.   Pott 4to,   pages, 16 Full-page Illus-
trations and New Title-page and Cover Designs.   Price 5s.
net.

The Literary Contributions by WILLIAM WATSON, H. D.
TRAILL, RICHARD LE GALLIENNE, ELLA D'ARCY, ROSA-
MUND MARRIOTT-WATSON, KENNETH GRAHAME, HENRY
HARLAND, DAUPHIN MEUNIER, MRS. MURRAY HICKSON,
EDMUND GOSSE, CHARLES KENNETT BURROW, LEILA
MACDONALD, HUBERT CRACKANTHORPE, ERNEST WENT-
WORTH, C. S., G. S. STREET, NORA HOPPER, JAMES
ASHCROFT NOBLE, B. PAUL NEUMAN, EVELYN SHARP,
W. A. MACKENZIE, MRS. ERNEST LEVERSON, RICHARD
GARNETT, MAURICE BARING, NORMAN GALE, ANATOLE
FRANCE, and JOHN DAVIDSON.

The Art Contributions by E. A. WALTON, R. ANNING BELL,
ALFRED THORNTON, F. G. COTMAN, P. WILSON STEER,
A. S. HARTRICK, ROBERT HALLS, WALTER SICKERT,
CONSTANTIN GUYS, and AUBREY BEARDSLEY.

Prospectuses Post Free on Application.

LONDON : JOHN LANE
BOSTON : COPELAND & DAY